Messages from
HOLLOW

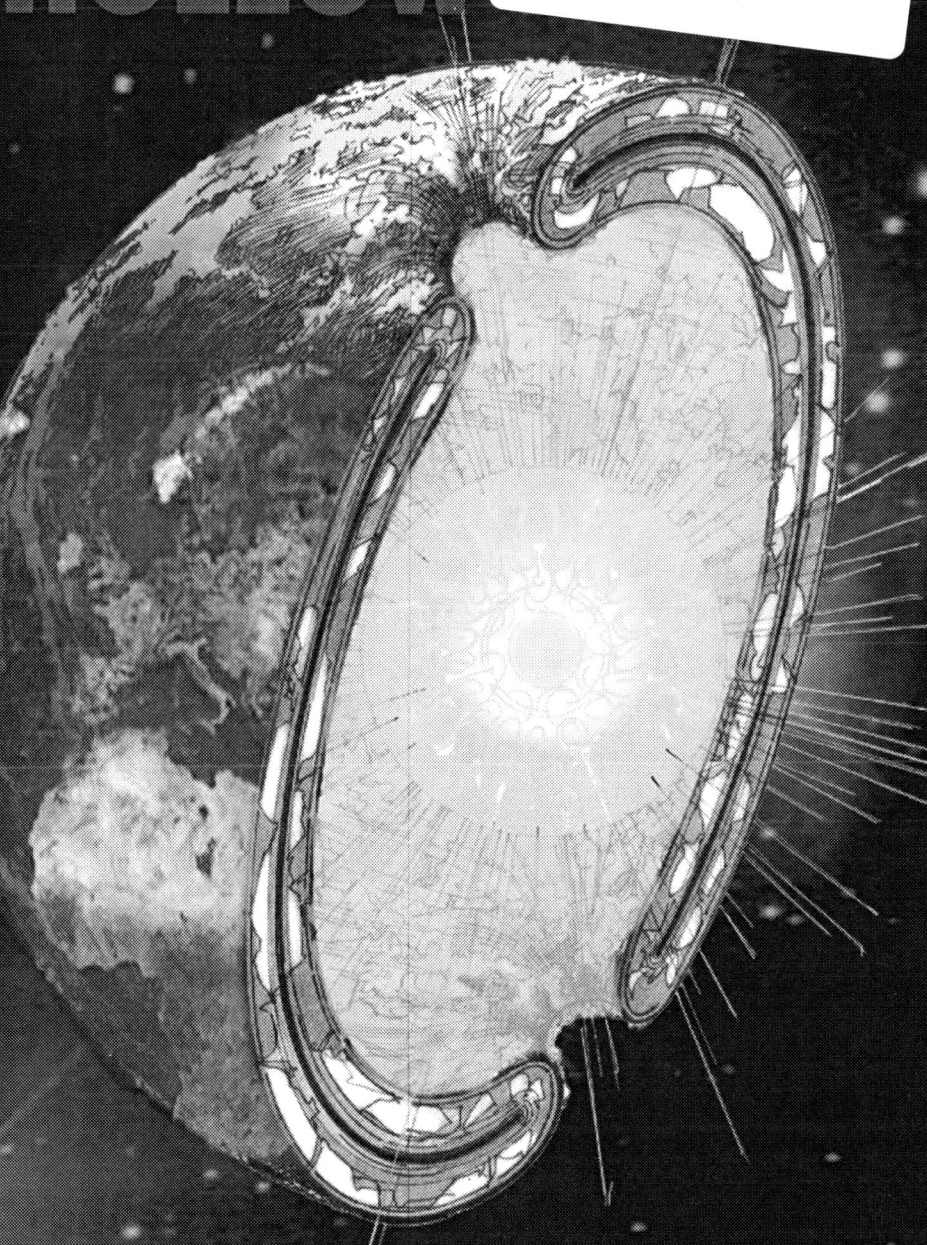

Dianne Robbins

© Copyright 2003 Dianne Robbins. All rights reserved.

I CLAIM EARTH'S COPYRIGHT
for these messages in the name of Mikos. The channeled messages in this book contain Spiritual Truths For the elevation of human consciousness.
SPIRITUAL TRUTH IS FREE:
It is our birthright! *Messages from the Hollow Earth* is published and distributed by: Dianne Robbins
Box 10945
Rochester, NY   14610-0945 USA
585.802.4530
HollowEarth@photon.net
$18
Postage: $4 USA, $4 Canada, $7 international

National Library of Canada Cataloguing in Publication Data

Robbins, Dianne, 1939-
    Messages from the hollow earth / Dianne Robbins.
ISBN 1-4120-0529-9
    I. Title.
PS3618.O22M48 2003   813'.6   C2003-903310-4

TRAFFORD

This book was published *on-demand* in cooperation with Trafford Publishing.
On-demand publishing is a unique process and service of making a book available for retail sale to the public taking advantage of on-demand manufacturing and Internet marketing.
On-demand publishing includes promotions, retail sales, manufacturing, order fulfilment, accounting and collecting royalties on behalf of the author.

Suite 6E, 2333 Government St., Victoria, B.C. V8T 4P4, CANADA
Phone   250-383-6864   Toll-free   1-888-232-4444 (Canada & US)
Fax   250-383-6804   E-mail   sales@trafford.com
Web site www.trafford.com   TRAFFORD PUBLISHING IS A DIVISION OF TRAFFORD HOLDINGS LTD.
Trafford Catalogue #03-0898   www.trafford.com/robots/03-0898.html

1 0   9   8   7   6   5   4

Dedication

*In deepest Love and Gratitude
I dedicate this book to my Eternal Friend*
Mikos
*from the Library of Porthologos
inside the HOLLOW EARTH.*

In Appreciation

Eric Karagounis, who also channels Mikos, and assists me with the distribution of my Telos book. San Francisco, CA Skarfia@aol.com

Noelle and Masaru Takahashi, originators of the "Patterns of Light" tools and techniques for transformation for the New Era. Salinas, CA 831.449.2467 NoelleNow@earthlink.net

Martin L. K., for assistance with my Telos book. Sausalito, California.

Edward Rice, Multidimensional Healer & 21st Century Shaman. Santa Fe, NM, www.edwardrice.com 505.989.4131

Richard Bryant, Medical Intuitive, Healer, Geomancer and Teacher. Founder of the Freeman School in Portland, Oregon, www.adinfinitum.org 503.493.4245

Rakesh Maniktala, Haridwar, India, on the foothills of the Himalayas. www.geocities.com/ancientscience

Acknowledgements

A very special thanks to
Lawrence Frank
Who has come forth to assist me in the publication of
my books. His immense support has made these messages
from the world below available to the world above.

To Suzanne Mattes Bennett
For the Welcoming message from Mikos.

To Eric Karagounis
For contributing his message from Mikos.

To James Michaelson
For permission to use his original artwork
as the basis for my book cover design.

To Greg Gavin
For his graphic and technical skills
in helping me design my book cover.

To my mother Selma
A rare combination of wisdom, love and graciousness
that overflows abundantly to all.

To my grandson Ryan
The Center of My Universe.

To Patricia Mannix
For her help in formatting this book.

The messages in this book contain Spiritual Truths
for the elevation of human consciousness
and may be copied and disseminated
without permission by the author.

"Open yourselves up to the existence of other life
existing beside you on your home planet
and you will be able to explore all the wonders
that truly do exist inside this globe you call Earth."
Mikos

"These messages are from people actually living inside the Hollow Earth, and they bring to life all the research I've done and the books I've published." Timothy Green Beckley, President, Global Communications.

"There is more to this planet than meets the eye. This book contains a description of a world within a world that has been spoken of by writers such as John Uri Lloyd, Raymond Bernard, John Cleves Symmes, and Edgar Rice Burroughs. In the messages in this book, the description of this world comes from those who would know the most...those who actually live there." BRANTON, Hollow Earth Researcher.

"This book offers a personal insight into the realm of the Inner Earth. In my own experiences with the Inner Earth, I saw myself in a vast library, which contained among other sources, the entire contents of the ancient Library of Alexandria. In this book, Dianne also talks about an inner earth library called "Porthologos", which Mikos said contained the contents of the Library of Alexandria. This certainly is a touch point we share in our experience of the Inner Earth." Rev. Maia Christianne+, Akashic Translator and Digital Spirit Artist. Spirit Heart Sanctuary.

"Explore at depth the lifestyle and society
of another advanced civilization
that already reached the ascended state
of consciousness that is our human destiny."
Mikos

Contents

1. Introduction
- 10   Preface
- 11   A Word from the Author
- 13   Explanation of our Hollow Earth
- 16   Drawing of Hollow Earth, by Max Fyfield
- 17   Introduction from Adama
- 19   Welcome (through Suzanne Mattes Bennett)
- 21   You Have Waited Thousands of Years

2. The Library of Porthologos
- 23   Holds the Records of the Universe
- 23   Guides the Evolution of the Planet
- 24   Purpose of Library of Porthologos
- 26   Inter-Dimensional Portal

3. Our Galactic Connection
- 30   Story of the Hollow Earth Inhabitants
- 31   We Once Lived on Another Solar System
- 33   All Planets Have Openings
- 34   Adama Talks About Inner Earth Beings

4. Space Portals and Travel
- 36   We Travel Through Our Portals
- 36   We Travel Freely Inside Our Globe
- 37   We Come and Go Through the Poles
- 39   Our Portals Lead to All Star Systems
- 41   Portal to the Sun
- 42   Spaceports Inside the Earth

5. Free Energy and Abundance
- 44   Earth Provides Free Sources of Energy
- 45   Harmony Restores the Flow of Abundance

6. Technology
    47   Our Technology Advances our Civilization
    48   Electrons Remain Intact in our Water
    49   We Store Our Records on Telonium Plates

7. Uncovering Our Existence
    50   We Are The Diamonds and You are the Miners
    51   Porthologos is in a Huge, Carved Out Cavity
    52   Our Haven Underground

8. Time, Telepathy, and Consciousness
    58   Time is Determined by Level of Consciousness
    60   You Have More than Five Senses
    62   There is No Delay in Telepathic Transmissions
    64   Telepathy
    65   You Are the Knower of All

9. Cures for Pollution and Diseases
    66   Once Your Pollution is Cleared Up
    67   Cure for All Diseases Already Exists
    68   Protect Your Newborn
    69   A Great Dispensation Has Just Been Granted

10. Evolution is the Solution, 9-11-2001
    72   911 Was Call for Help
    73   Inner Planes Electoral Vote
    76   We Monitor the Milky Way Galaxy
    77   Sleeping Giants of Yore
    79   European Euro
    80   Confusion and Turmoil on the Surface
    81   Peace Is the Answer

11. Our Immortality
    83   We Don't Age
    85   We Have the Eyes of Falcons
    85   Frequently Asked Questions

12. Our Oceans and Beaches
    88   Our Water is Alive with Consciousness
    89   Our Water Talks
    91   Inner Earth Sanctuaries to all Marine Life

13. Food and Elements of Nature
    93   Earth Gives All Life a Home to Evolve On
    95   Food Takes on the Mass Consciousness
    99   Our Fields of Grains

14. Our Environment and Weather
    101   How do you Control the Weather?
    103   Oceans and Mountains
    104   Our Weather, Tunnels and Spaceports
    106   Tunnel Map

15. Our Homes
    107   Our Buildings are Round
    107   Jewels, Diamonds, and Crystals
    109   We Live Inside Caverns
    111   Inner Earth Caverns - Humanity's New Home

16. DNA and Inner Doors of Consciousness
    113   All People are from the Same DNA Blueprint
    115   Feel Your Heart As It Beats
    115   Living Library of Knowledge is Within You

17. Synchronicity, Imagination, and Rebirth
    119 Synchronicity and Unity Consciousness
    122 Your Internal Light
    123 Imagination is the Substance of the Universe
    125 Spring of Rebirth
    126 A New Golden Age
    128 Return of Christ Consciousness

18. The Earth and Crystals
    130 Our Earth Herself is a Crystal
    132 Everything is Constructed of Crystals
    137 Earth is Showcase of Milky Way Galaxy

19. Confederation of Planets
    140 We Are an Arm of the Creator
    141 The Great Rebirthing
    142 Are All Planets Hollow?
    142 Our Computer System Links Us
    143 We Trees are the Ground Crew

20. Ascension
    145 Earth Shifting into Higher Dimensions
    146 All Life Forms Opting for Ascension
    147 Timelines for Earth's Ascension
    148 Solar Flares
    148 Critical Mass
    151 Quickening the Soul
    152 Love is the Key

21. Reunion-A Journey in Consciousness
    154 Your Journey Home
    155 Drama in Optical Illusion
    156 Message to Dianne
    158 Crossing Over Dimensions

22. How To Connect With Us
    159 Universal Linkage
    159 We Have Established a Link
    160 Points of Emergence
    163 We Hope You Will Hasten to Our Call

23. Earth's Glorious Future
    165   Stick Around (through Eric Karagounis)

24. Addendum
    167 About the City of Telos
    169 Secrets of the Subterranean Cities
    175 The Ashtar Galactic Command
    179 The Smoky God
    180 Admiral Richard Byrd's Flight
    184 Telos: Hollow Earth & Underground Cities
    186 The Call Goes Out: Earth's Cetaceans
    188 About the Author
    190 Credit for Original Book Cover Design

25. Resources
    191 Hollow Earth Researchers
    191 Hollow Earth Books
    193 Hollow Earth Websites
    195 Maia's Image of Mikos
    196 Spirit-Art
    197 Greg's Drawing of Mikos
    198 Portrait of Adama

1. Introduction

Preface

Not too long ago humanity believed that the world was flat and that the Sun revolved around the Earth. Humanity was so sure of this that it became an established 'fact'.

When Galileo presented evidence that proved the Earth revolved around the Sun, he was not only ridiculed but he was imprisoned because his findings were such a radical departure from accepted thought.

A similar situation exists today with the new revelation that the Earth is HOLLOW at its core. Hollow Earth Researchers* have presented evidence, based on their research of how planets are formed, that our Earth is not solid as our textbooks have taught us to believe.

This book is about the greatest revelation in history by stating that not only is the Earth's core Hollow, but it is INHABITED by highly evolved human beings who are communicating their existence to us.

Will humanity be open to this new revelation about the Earth, or will they ridicule it because it is not in our textbooks?

Lawrence Frank
March 3, 2003

*Information about Hollow Earth Researchers can be found in chapter 25.

A Word from the Author

In the early 1990's, I read a newsletter* about a woman named Sharula, who was born in Telos, a Subterranean City located beneath Mt. Shasta, California, and who came to our surface in the 1960's. She now lives in Santa Fe, New Mexico with her husband Shield. In the years before moving to Santa Fe, she was known in the Mt. Shasta area as Bonnie.

In Sharula's newsletter, she wrote about life in Telos and about the other Subterranean Cities that exist beneath the Earth's surface*. She wrote about the Ascended Master and High Priest of Telos, named Adama. Shortly after my reading about Adama, he contacted me telepathically and asked me if I would take his messages. *You see, our thoughts go out into the Universe and instantly connect us to whomever we think about.*

Adama began to dictate messages to me and some of his messages were about their connection to the Hollow Earth, which created an 'opening' for me to receive messages from Mikos, who lives in the city of Catharia, located beneath the Aegean Sea, inside the Hollow Earth. Those messages from Adama and Mikos were published in 2000, in my second book entitled *TELOS: The Call Goes Out from the HOLLOW EARTH and the UNDERGROUND CITIES*.

After my TELOS book (messages from both Adama in Telos and some messages from Mikos) was published, I was talking to Adama one day, when Mikos got on the line. It was a 3-way conference call. Mikos asked if I would take more messages from him, and publish them in another book of messages exclusively from the Hollow Earth. *Messages from the Hollow Earth* is the sequel to my TELOS book. It contains all the new messages that I have been receiving from Mikos in the three years since the TELOS publication. It goes down deeper and explores further the cavity of the

Earth, illuminating the other civilizations that reside inside our hollow planet. Its thrust is to bring you the reader, to its innermost core, where you can explore at depth the lifestyle and society of another advanced civilization that already reached the ascended state of consciousness that is our human destiny.

Over the centuries our perception and knowledge have greatly expanded regarding the nature of the universe. Modern astronomy has shown our solar system to be 'just another one' in the arms of our Milky Way Galaxy…which in turn is just one of the billions of galaxies in this vast and expanding universe. Advent of time, and progress of science have broken many myths. **Now is the time for breaking yet another MYTH – that of a solid Earth.**

* The information I read about Sharula and Telos in the newsletter is in chapter 24.

Explanation of our Hollow Earth

Not just our Earth, but all planets are hollow! Planets are formed by hot gases thrown from a sun into an orbit, and the shell of planets is created by gravity and centrifugal forces and the POLES REMAIN OPEN and lead to a hollow interior. This process forms a hollow sphere with an Inner Sun, smoky in color, which gives off soft and pleasant full spectrum sunlight, making the inside surface highly conducive to growth of vegetation and human life…with only a long-long day and no nights.

The **HOLLOW EARTH BEINGS** are very spiritually evolved and technologically advanced, and live inside the interior core of our Hollow Earth. These advanced civilizations live in peace and brotherhood in the Center of our Earth, which contains an Inner Central Sun, with oceans and mountains still in their pristine state.

The Hollow Earth cavity is still in its pristine state because they don't walk or build upon their land. There are no buildings, shopping malls or highways. They travel in electromagnetic vehicles that levitate a few inches above ground. They walk along streams, rivers, and oceans and climb mountains – but that's the extent of their foot contact with the ground. They leave the rest of their land to nature, because it's nature's land too.

The governing city within the Hollow Earth is called Shamballa. It is located inside the very center of the planet, and can be accessed through the holes at either the North or South poles. The Northern and Southern Lights that we see in our skies are actually reflections from our Hollow Earth's Inner Central Sun, which emanates from her hollow core.

They use free energy to light up their cities, homes, and tunnels. They use crystals, coupled with electromagnetism, which generates a small sun with full-spectrum lighting that lasts for half a million years, and gives them all the power they need.

The Earth's crust is approximately 800 miles from the outer to the inner surface. Because our Earth is hollow, and not a solid sphere, the center of gravity is not in the center of the Earth, but in the center of its crust, which is 400 miles below the surface.

The source of Earth's magnetic field has been a mystery. The Inner Sun at the center of Earth is the mysterious power source behind the Earth's magnetic field.

There are entry caverns all over the Earth, where interactions can take place. Only some are currently open. Nikola Tesla, the genius inventor of electrical technology, is now living inside the Hollow Earth. He began to receive information in the latter part of the 1800's and discovered that: "electric power is everywhere present in unlimited quantities and can drive the world's machinery without the need of coal, oil, gas or any other of the common fuels." In the 1930's the tunnel entrances and passageways were closed off by the Hollow Earth civilizations because 'corporations' at that time were misusing Tesla's technology to gain entrance into the Inner Earth. The Hollow Earth's two main portals are at the Holes at the Poles, which were closed off in the year 2000 because our governments were setting detonations at the Poles to blow open entrances into their world. They have installed a magnetic force field around Earth's polar openings to further camouflage the entrances. This way, the openings are protected from air and land sightings. In the past there were entrances to the Library of Porthologos on the surface. One such entrance was the Library of Alexandria, which was destroyed by fire in A.D. 642.

There is more landmass inside (3/4 land and 1/4 water) and the land is more condensed than ours. Everything in the Hollow Earth is very carefully maintained to balance the ecological system of all life forms that reside there.

There are several million Catharians currently residing in the Hollow Earth. There are Catharians who have incarnated as humans on the surface. There are also Catharians that live on the planet Jupiter. The tallest Catharian is 23 feet tall. There are 36,000 humans from our surface who now live inside the Earth. Over the last 200 years approximately 50 surface humans went inside to live. Over the last 20 years only 8 went inside to live.

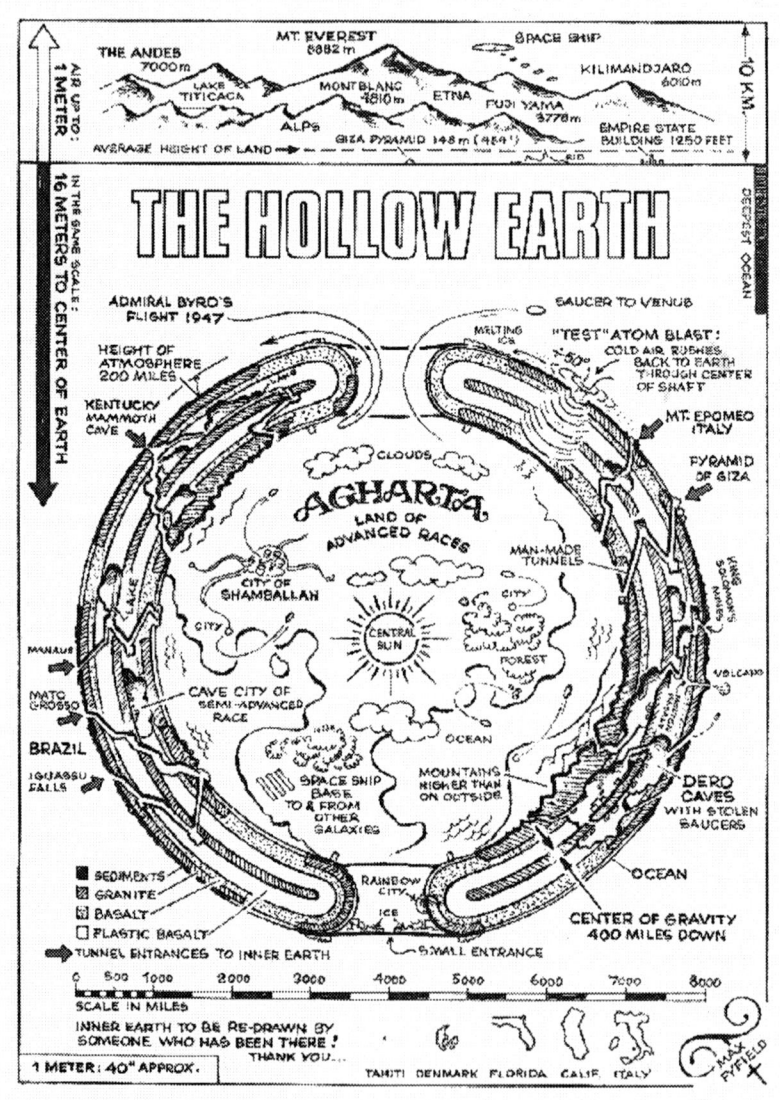

Reproduced by permission of copyright owner, Max Fyfield, Ordrup Jagtvej 71, 2920 Charlottenlund, Denmark.

Introduction from Adama

I am Adama, and I greet you from the Subterranean City of TELOS, located beneath Mt. Shasta in California, where our Lemurian colony currently dwells. We are in great anticipation of the publication of this new book of messages from the Hollow Earth, which is located in the very center of our planet.

I would like to introduce a great historian to you, Mikos of Catharia, who is intrinsically linked to the great Library of Porthologos, formerly known in your history books as the Library of Alexandria, where all your Earth's records are kept.

Mikos, by nature, is a most gentle soul, and he and I have been residing on this Earth plane for eons of time. We have traveled extensively together, attended more council meetings together than you can count, and have spent time together in each other's homes and cities. We, in the Subterranean City of Telos, work intimately with Mikos and his entourage in Catharia, and we spend much of our time, when we are visiting the Hollow Earth, in the great Library of Porthologos, where we continue our learning in the vastness of its portals.

We want you to know that our connection to each other is as one link on a fence. We in Telos work as one with our brothers and sisters in Catharia, as our mission is to bring the Earth and surface humanity into her ascension. Although our civilizations are based on the same Divine Laws of Creation, our experiences as a culture differ, due to our different geographical locations on Earth. But this is our only difference, and makes our interactions more fruitful as we each bring different riches to the table of our council meetings.

Mikos has been a close friend and companion traveler of mine for eons of Earth time, and we work together closely to join all the civilizations on and in Earth together into one United Earth-World Colony, so that our planet will be readied to make the great trip with the rest of our Milky Way Galaxy into a higher state of evolution. Our location in our new position in the Milky Way Galaxy has been prepared and is waiting for us all to return home to.

As you read the pages in this book, your heart will be prepared to make the journey with us into our new home of Light everlasting. We beckon you to travel with us through these pages of great insight and delight, and learn the true history of your planet Earth, and how other civilizations live embedded beneath your surface and below your periphery of vision.

Our TELOS book is a pre-requisite to this sequel, in terms of establishing our Telosian history and lifestyle as contrasted to that of the Hollow Earth inhabitants, who are only a step below us. We are all ONE and the same, and yet different in myriad ways; just as your nations and people are on the surface. Both of our civilizations chose to live underground in isolation from the surface population, so we could evolve in tranquility and peace.

So ride with us in your thoughts, and travel to the innermost depths of our Earth, and you will find the lost Garden of Eden your bible talks about. It is right here, in the center of your Earth, waiting to be explored by you, the reader. We welcome you in. I am Adama.

Welcome
(*Mikos*, through Suzanne Mattes Bennett)

Welcome! Welcome to the beginning of a marvelous, and for many a seemingly unbelievable journey. My name is Mikos, and you are about to enter through these pages a realm that predates history as you know it. A realm of fancy and fantasy, a realm of surrealistic beauty and eternal changelessness; a place that has been hidden to all but a few souls who have ventured here in the past by invitation only.

For some, this journey presented revelations beyond time. For all, it changed the course of their understanding in the world in which they lived, and ultimately their entire lives. In reading the humble messages of these pages which lie before you, you are about to meet one of those people, Dianne Robbins…a beautiful, gracious, and the gentlest of souls, whose life is intimately connected and bound together with the Cetacean life which reside beneath the waters of your world.

What you are about to read is no less a miracle, one which many years from now will bear the finest and richest of fruits. The fruit of knowledge…the fruit of gentle wisdom… the fruit of truth, unity, compassion, and endless joy and love… by which life was always meant to flourish.

Please accept this invitation now and begin a journey into the mysterious world in which I live. Welcome to the Hollow Earth. My people welcome you with Joy, Love, and Peacefulness. May all your journeys in literature be as wondrous and beautiful as the information that lies before you now.

Welcome, dearest children. Welcome to the Library of Porthologos, where the history of all dimensions are shared, stored, and preserved. Where nothing is lost and where every life that has ever existed has been woven into the meaning in the tapestry. Our world is one in which no item as small, or as seemingly insignificant, has been overlooked. This is a Library…a Library nestled beneath the long, deep silence of the Aegean Sea. We, who live and work here, welcome you.

Welcome to the world that awaits your discovery, not only in literature, in written text, but also in form, where through us and a limitless supply of imagination can bring to life the greatest minds that have ever existed. Nothing is lost here.

You can meet and interact with all of creation when you enter through our doors.

You are about to enter a Library…
The Lost City…
The Library of Alexandria!

You Have Waited Thousands of Years to Hear Our Messages

Greetings from the Hollow Earth! I am Mikos and I dwell inside your Earth. I am reaching up to you in consciousness, to impart our frequency to you as you read the words on these pages of our book. These pages are sacred, for its content contains the mighty power to change the world – if but enough surface folk read them. This is our purpose for dictating our messages to you. It is to hasten change on the surface so that people will once again be connected to their divine self and source of inner guidance.

You have waited for thousands of years to hear our messages, and it is only now that the vibration is high enough for us to come forward and speak to you. These messages you read, come directly through our hearts, relayed from the heart of God. Your heart is God's receptacle – so open it wide, my dear readers, and receive our words directly into your heart – where their vibrations will raise your consciousness enough to meld into us directly as your eyes perceive our words.

We await the great day when we will be able to show our selves to you, when you will be able to peer directly into our eyes and fathom the God within our souls – including yours. Many are now still separated from the Lord God I AM of their being, but our purpose for these messages is to bring you the reality of your own God Selves and help you connect to the Light within your own soul.

Life is about connecting – not disconnecting into separate units, as your density and negativity and limitation on the surface caused you to do. Life is a flow of energy, connecting everyone, everywhere, simultaneously. We invite you to be in this flow, and flow with our thoughts and our heartbeat as you read our words carried to the surface on the winds of telepathy – winds that bring our thoughts and feelings into your heartspace – for you to also access as you learn to resonate with our vibration. As you think of Us, you will feel a heightened sense of being as our energy cascades into you. It is a physical sensation that is unmistakable. Move into it – for it is Us – making contact with you – consciousness contact – and it feels like energy currents flowing through you, currents of heightened sensitivity and divine bliss, putting you into a protected space of peace during our connection, that lingers about you for the remaining day. We offer you this, as a gift freely given as you read our words. We've been calling to you for so long, and now through this book to the world, you are hearing us. We are joyously anticipating your heart contact and are ready and eager to respond to your thoughts. So tune into us, sit quietly, and feel our vibration engulf your physical body and raise your energy field. We wait for your call.

2. The Library of Porthologos

Our Library Holds the Records of the Universe
Greetings from the Center of the Earth! My name is Mikos, and I am a resident of the city of Catharia. I am talking to you from the Library of Porthologos, located in the Hollow Earth beneath the Aegean Sea.

I am very old by definition. I span eons of time in the same body. I have been able to compile Earth's records in the Library of Porthologos, where all Earth's history has been preserved. Our library is immense and extensive, and holds the records of the Universe – not just Earth. We can study the history of all planets and solar systems and learn everything about life everywhere. Such is our library's capacity. Not only can we read about it, but we can experience it all firsthand from our crystals that store the memories of all events. So we can access these events, learn from them, and solve our problems easily and with the best possible outcomes for all involved.

Our Library Guides the Evolution of a Planet
I am a librarian and researcher by trade, but a statesman (although we have no states) and ambassador for the whole Earth. I venture out on journeys to other star systems and galaxies and arrange for their records to be transferred to our library here in Porthologos for safekeeping. We house all the records in our Universe so that some day all people, everywhere in our Universe, will be able to come here to peruse their records and learn their wisdom to avert the negative and ensure the positive outcome of all events. This is the purpose of a library – it is to give guidance for the evolution of a society and a planet so that the people can live and evolve in peace and prosperity – not negativity and war.

All conceivable situations and answers are found in our library, ready to be assimilated by you. As soon as peace prevails on the surface, we can open our library doors to you and accompany you inside. We long for this day, which is assuredly dawning. As we draw closer to our glorious reunion, we send you our everlasting love from below and hope you will return it on your out-breath, where we can set up a circle of love revolving around and through our beloved Earth. I am Mikos, love incarnate.

The Purpose of the Library of Porthologos

I am Guardian of the Earth's records, and all records in your Solar System and Universe. I am here, in the cavity of Earth, primarily to guard the history of all life everywhere. This is our prime purpose and the purpose for the Library of Porthologos.

Our library is the only one of its kind in our vast system of planets. Our library is so vast that it covers 456 square miles of terrain and has vast storage vaults containing records all stored on crystal slides that are viewed through our crystal projectors. Our storage facilities are vast, organized and categorized, so that you can easily locate the information you are looking for and retrieve it for viewing. We have vast conveyers that will deliver your order within minutes, and then return it back to its storage location again. This way, every item in the library is always where it should be and can be easily found and perfectly preserved. Such is our technological capabilities. For we have drawn on the technology of the Universe we reside in, and have the most advanced methods of preservation and storage and retrieval that would marvel your library systems beyond anything you could dream of.

For we don't have dead books on our shelves—**we have living records of life, in all its vast and differentiated forms of existence, that play out its story as on a live stage in a theatre; and we sit and view it, as if we're in the**

audience, thus having this first hand experience of all history right here and now. It is truly a marvel to witness, and the most evolved way to learn about life in all its varied forms.

There are these mini-theatres all throughout the library, where we can sit in comfort and view any activity or event we choose that has taken place on Earth and in our Universe throughout all time. This is really what theatre is about, with live actors portraying themselves, as they were, at that particular event in time. This is the best way to learn about life in our Galaxy, and makes history come alive and jump out at you and capture your attention and you become part of it and feel it and experience it. It is the best way to learn.

Your surface Earth history classes are dull and boring compared to our way of learning, and accounts for your loss of attention and loss of interest in your school classrooms—aside from the fact that your information is misinformation based on someone's theory or prejudice, rather than actual fact. You would like our library and would find learning exciting and wondrous to experience.

Someday, you will be able to access all the information in the Library of Porthologos, when you travel here through the tunnel system that will be open between our two civilizations in the future when surface humans stop warring and people reach Unity Consciousness. Then the world will open up to you and you will experience the joy and freedom of being in unity with All of Us in this Universe, and will benefit from all our wisdom and all our accomplishments. This is how planets, solar systems, galaxies and universes evolve—by uniting in one consciousness and evolving together through Eternity—one step at a time, climbing the Spiral of Evolution together, and bringing everyone along so that all evolve and all benefit and no-one is left behind. Unity Consciousness carries us all, so that all life advances according to its divine plan, and all life is in harmony with its home planet. This is the best way to evolve, and we highly recommend it to you.

The Light is expanding in your mass consciousness and soon you will feel its intensity which will drastically move your vibration into the higher octaves where the frequency will bring you all into Unity Consciousness without your realizing it. One day, you will just open your eyes and you will be there—and be with us– and marvel at it all. It will seem as magic to you and seem as if it always was; and all the suffering of the past will be obliterated and erased from your cells and you will rejoice at finding yourself at last. We will enfold you in our arms, and we, too, will rejoice in reuniting with you, our brothers and sisters, at long last. I am Mikos, your friend from the past.

The Library of Porthologos is an Interdimensional Portal

Good morning. I am Mikos, and my entourage and I have been awaiting you on the doorstep to the Library of Porthologos, where the white alabaster steps twinkle with the sparks of embedded crystals and diamonds, leading into the great halls of our library located inside the Earth's vast interior.

Today we will take you on a tour through our halls, and show you what a true library in your future will look like. Your future libraries will look like ours, as ours is the model that all libraries will replicate. We will start with the outer grounds, as there are inner grounds too. The outer grounds are lush with grasses, flowers, bushes and trees; and there are circular clearings with soft benches and lounging chairs in the center, accompanied by small, round, tall tables to set your accouterments on. There are small springs of waterfalls and fountains in these enclosures, for our water is alive and in a full state of consciousness that sings. Yes, *our water sings*, and as you lounge in our secluded enclosure you are sung to by the water of life, as it sprays from our fountains with melodies of deep love that harmonizes and balances all the cells in your body. From this state of deep peacefulness and harmony, we sit and relax at intervals during our 'work' day.

And now we go inside the Library of Porthologos, and walk up the crystal staircase, where the door opens up into the Universe. Yes, the Library is multidimensional! As you enter, you see the Milky Way Galaxy floating around you, and can glance into the heavens beyond, which encompasses our whole Universe. You see the stars and suns and other solar systems revolving around our Central Sun; and you feel part of 'All That Is', as indeed you are.

And yes, there is more. The Library of Porthologos is an Interdimensional Portal that can take you to wherever you project your thoughts and intentions to go and see 'first hand'. Yes, it is magic on the surface, but here it is natural and real and accepted as part of life, as indeed it is. It allows our eyes to see the wonders of life that surrounds us, not just a blank, dark, or cloudy sky overhead, interspersed with tiny, far distant stars, that your surface folk hardly look up to anymore, as their gaze is directed more to their ground struggle for survival.

So, we are fully inside now, and you witness the wonders of our Universe through your inner sight, which now becomes your natural outer sight. As you begin to walk through the door, magic enfolds you, and magical sights, sounds and senses embrace you. You are fully energized and vibrant, and your cells sing to the sounds of the crystals embedded throughout the library, for our library is all crystals and jewels, all in harmony, and all in tune, carrying the rhythm and beat of the Earth, the Milky Way Galaxy, and Universe. Your cells chime to this universal beat. Ah, you are in ecstasy! There is color and light all around you, and all the Beings you meet radiate this great light and unconditional love coming from the core of our Central Sun directly into the heart of the library's portal. You feel this love intensely and are in love with all around you and in love with everyone, everywhere. You are truly 'alive' at last. You bless the flame of life within you, and proceed into the vastness of Porthologos.

You see people everywhere – walking, talking, studying, sitting, reclining, dreaming and just soaking in the vibrations of peace. Everywhere there are flowers of great vibrancy and fountains and pools of water spilling forth their choruses of song. You look around and see secluded alcoves interspersed throughout the vast halls, with the most ergonomically structured chairs beckoning you to recline upon them. You find one calling to you, and you sit down and experience a connection to this chair that tunes you to its vibration so that you are connected to the mainframe of the internal computer in the library. You are, so to speak, 'wired up' with the wireless wires, and fully connected to the operating system, which you operate with your <u>thoughts</u> and <u>feelings</u>, and which will take you anywhere you 'wish' to go in our galaxy. You navigate with your mind, using your thoughts as your directional compass for coordinates of latitude and longitude. And it is so natural that you marvel at its simplicity and naturalness. And <u>you travel</u> in consciousness, and explore our Galaxy and Universe 'first hand' and for the first time in your fully conscious human state.

This is yet another aspect of what our library offers to its visitors, along with its crystal slides of all recorded history of our entire Universe. And *you are here* through the vibrational frequency of our words, as you read them and envision the sights in your 'imagination'. We welcome you, and invite you to enter at any time. Just call to us for entry, as our call is always going out to you. I AM MIKOS, and I am here to guide you personally through our library whenever you call. You don't need a 'library card', as your identification is inscribed in the DNA of your cells. We await your visit.

3. Our Galactic Connection

The Story of the Hollow Earth Inhabitants

Greetings from the Center of the Earth. I am Mikos, an inhabitant below the Earth's surface, enfolded in the hollow globe deep on the inside space of Earth, as lifeforms circle around and above us on the surface. You are on the rim, so to speak, while we dwell in the cradle, which is safe and secure from outside forces of chaos that are currently raging around you.

As many of you are now familiar with Telos, but not really familiar with the Hollow Earth inhabitants, we would like you to hear our story now. We are a very advanced race of Beings who have never resided on the surface. We have come from other planets in your solar system and other galaxies from the far out reaches of space. We came here to oversee the Earth, and we came here to continue our own evolution without interference from any race or ET's. We are securely encased in the core of the Earth, sufficiently to protect us from all outside intrusion, so that we can evolve as quickly as we can in order to secure this planet as an outpost of Love and Light. For the quicker we can evolve, the quicker we can come to the surface to help struggling humanity gain its freedom into the Light of God's Love. This is why you have not seen or heard from us. It is because we have self-imposed this seclusion.

We now wish you to acknowledge Us, standing free in the Light of God, in the midst of you; constantly radiating out our Light and Love to you to grasp and hold onto as we pull you closer and closer to our heart's flame, until you meld with us into God's mighty stream of Light, enabling you to then go forth into the world, where you'll shine as a beacon, and where all who encounter your radiance become magnetized from within to begin their transformation in consciousness and increased awareness of the multitudes of Beings who are here to help you and all life on Earth to evolve into higher and higher states of consciousness until all of Earth, together, explodes into her ascension of Light, and all are freed of Earth's density forever.

This is our role, this is our final goal to carry out on Earth, and then we will all, en masse, move up the spiral of evolution into the realm of Light and Love, and become who we truly are, living in a place of peace, beauty and prosperity, together as one cell in God's heart. So make this journey into Light with us, by opening your hearts to our existence and welcoming us into your life, so that we too, may guide you onto the steps of continual glory, where we step with you, side by side, on our path to God. So walk with us, hand in hand, and whenever you're weary, think of us holding you and supporting you as we all, as a planet, move closer and closer to our ascension. You are close, very close, and we are here to give you that extra push into the Light, where we all await your presence.

We bask in the Light of the Hollow Earth, where we have created a paradise within the womb of Mother Earth. And, we wish you, too, to experience this paradise along with us. We are now working closely with you, our brothers and sisters on the surface, and we cheer you on. I am Mikos, your friend from the past.

We Once Lived on Another Solar System

Greetings, my fellow travelers on Earth! It is Mikos, speaking to you today from inside the Hollow Earth, which is our home. We have been here for millions of years, slowly evolving ourselves into the God Beings that we are. Our evolution has made great strides due to the isolation of being wrapped up inside the womb of Mother Earth.

All our lives have been spent in peace and bliss, due to our location. We exist here in peace and tranquility because of the proximity to the heartbeat of Mother Earth. The more deeply one goes into the Earth, the more deeply one feels the beat of the Earth. And the more one feels Her heartbeat, the more one resonates to her Goddess qualities. So this proximity has led Us, over the millennia, to our oneness with all life and to our joy of existence. All life knows this oneness, yet most of life has yet to feel it in their outer bodies.

As the heartbeat of Mother Earth reverberates through the Earth, it reaches the surface, where you can feel and experience it. However, in order to feel and resonate with this beat of life, you have to be in peace. Your outer bodies have to be in coordination and in synchronicity with each other, all vibrating at the same velocity and all feeling the grace of God and immersion in the oneness of Creation. When your bodies are at rest, at night, they resonate to the deep beat within them. **You can only evolve when you are in a state of peace.** And this is why We, who are immersed in Earth's depths, have been able to evolve; because We have been in synchronicity with the beat of all life and with Our selves.

Once we were adrift in space, living on another solar system in the Milky Way Galaxy. At that time, there were what you today call "Star Wars." People were engaged in battles to control our section of the galaxy. These battles brought great destruction to planets and knocked solar systems off course. It was a dark time for our galaxy, and beings like ourselves yearned for peace to be restored so that we could continue our evolution. This is when We discovered the Earth.

We left our solar system and traveled here, which at the time was a planet little known outside its parameter. When We alighted on the surface, we were amazed and in awe of the beauty and tranquility of Earth. We explored the surface and found the open tunnels leading into the cavity inside. These were already existing tunnels from other civilizations, for the Earth is very old and her civilizations ancient.

All Planets Have Openings at Their North and South Poles

We migrated through the poles and found our "nest" inside. The inside is so clean, so pure, and so peaceful, that from that time on we never left it.

Throughout the ages we have enlarged and expanded the tunnels leading to the Subterranean Cities and surface, as a means of travel for our inhabitants and yours. Although not too many surface travelers have used these tunnels, they exist for the future, when more of you and more of Us will intermingle and make the trip to visit each other. So the surface is dotted with tunnel entrances that you see on the map in this book, leading both to the Subterranean Cities and to Us. This is how it is on most planets in your galaxy, where people travel freely to both the cradle and the rim, to exchange information and to learn from each other.

Your Earth has quite a history, going back into millennia of time. Unfortunately, its history isn't always peaceful, because once it was discovered, people fought great wars trying to control it and mine and remove its precious resources. So know that these times of raping the Earth are over with. These beings are no longer allowed entry to this sector of the Galaxy, which is steadily rising in Light, even as the waves lap the shores. The Light is flowing ceaselessly now, and bringing the tranquility and awareness that all surface dwellers yearn for.

We, here in the Hollow recesses of the Earth, have been calling for eons for more Light and for help from the Confederation of Planets to intercede to stop the influx of ravaging bands of ET's who have been scouring space to find planets that are rich in reserves like Earth. But today it is done. Know that the Confederation fully protects this sector, so that life can finally begin to evolve in peace.

Adama Talks About the Inner Earth Beings Who Live in the Hollow Earth

We have easy access into the Inner Earth World through our tunnel system, which goes directly through the Earth's mantle and into the Inner Earth entryways, where we are greeted by our brothers and sisters upon our arrival. We are always going and coming, since we keep up a steady trade relation with them. We enjoy their beaches and oceans, and climb their mountains. It is a gloriously beautiful realm of Light and Purity, and truly invigorating to be there.

Know that the spiritual state of the Inner Earth Beings is very evolved compared to the surface dwellers. These Beings came from another solar system to populate the Inner Earth. They never lived on the surface. Their home on this planet has always been in the inner recesses of Earth. They are, however, in contact with Beings on the surface, just as you are in contact with Adama in the mantle.

You, on the surface, are the direct descendants of roving bands of ET's, who created you to mine the Earth's resources. These Creator ET's don't reside on Earth at this time. However, you all have the same Spiritual potential as Inner Earth Beings. Your life on the surface in no way mirrors life in the Inner Earth. The only things on the surface that mirror life inwardly are the mountains and oceans and plains.

These Inner Earth Beings have your surface conditions fully monitored. They know all that transpires on Earth, just as we in the mantle know all through our computer network.

The great Inner Earth Beings know of your yearnings to live in the Inner Earth, where all is in a peaceful, harmonious state. They do consider surface folk their brothers and sisters who have not as yet evolved enough to reside with them in the "land of plenty". However, when you do reach a higher Spiritual state, then you, too, can live internally within Earth.

4. Space Portals and Travel

We Travel Through Our Portals
Our galaxy operates as one huge whole system, totally interconnected through an interstellar communication web. Through our portals located in the Library of Porthologos, we can contact anyone, or travel anywhere in our Universe and beyond.

We Travel Freely Inside Our Globe
My dear friends of the Earth: I am Mikos, and I speak to you from the Great Cavern under your cities. This cavern spans the whole circumference of the center of the Earth. Our lives here are blessed with abundance in every way you can think of. Were you to let your imagination roam the Stars, all you can conceive of and more, we are blessed with. All we can imagine, we can manifest for ourselves. Such is the nature and natural law that exists everywhere you go in our Galaxy.

We are all Free Beings, free to travel and free to remain inside our cherished Earth. You may think our living space is cramped, but it is spacious, as our population is few compared to your billions. We travel freely inside our globe, needing no passports. Our means of travel is non-polluting, using only electromagnetic conveyances and crystal power. Your governments on the surface use these also, while keeping the secret well hidden from your populace. With all the rolling blackouts in California, soon your people will wake up to the unlimited supply of solar and wind and water/hydrogen power.

We are free to come and go as we please, and we often leave our homes for short trips to other star systems. We seldom visit your surface cities, but prefer to view them on our computer screens. This is the safest and most comprehensive way to follow your activities worldwide.

We are always awake when you call to us, as we are attuned to your frequency and can instantly hear and feel your call. With over-brimming love in our hearts, we salute you for your dedication to our mission.

We Can Easily Come And Go Through The Openings At The Poles

Our Spaceport is located inside the Hollow Earth, in direct alignment with the openings at the North and South Poles. We are not stuck on the Earth as you are, but can leave whenever we desire. We are not limited in movement, and can travel throughout the Universe at will. There are no physical constraints, for we apply the Universal Laws of Energy and use the already existing highways throughout the Universe. We can't get lost, for all is mapped out and all is in constant communication with all in existence. We just tap into this 'live' network that is always broadcasting and move through it effortlessly.

We are not isolated from the rest of life in our Universe – you are. We are not restricted in movement – you are.

As we are here in the Center of Earth's interior, you are here with us in consciousness. For consciousness is a 'place' – a place more solid than your physical places. So yes, you sit on the surface at your desk taking this dictation, but in consciousness you are with us inside the Hollow Earth. You are literally in two places at once. Do you understand multidimensionality now? Now that you are in both places simultaneously, we will show you around 'our place'. As you scan our landscape, you will 'see' the openings of the Holes at the Poles. These openings are wide enough for some Mother Ships to enter. You can 'see' the Spaceport, spread out for hundreds of miles in a circle interspersed with flowers, grasses, bushes, trees and waterfalls. It does not look like your barren, concrete airports, devoid of life; but rather like a garden with space shuttles and starships nestled peacefully inside our world.

We hardly know when they come and go, as they do not emit any harsh sounds, and we hardly detect any sound when they land or take off. They are in complete harmony with our love vibration and move in silence. We can visually see their movements as they gracefully fly in and out through the Poles. But this is the extent of it. There is no disturbance in sound or vibration, and there is no pollution and no destruction of our environment. This is quite a contrast from your surface airports, isn't it?

And, we never have "crashes," since every component of our craft is monitored by our amino-acid computers, and we detect and correct any problem immediately. Our technology is so far advanced from yours, for we've had the opportunity of peaceful living conditions to continuously develop it for millennia, without a break in our life spans. This is why your Immortality is so crucial. The longer you live in the same body, the more you can develop your talents and technologies, and the more you can create and refine things, rather than stopping and starting over again in each succeeding lifetime. All this stopping and starting over and over again gets you nowhere. You are continuously 'reinventing the wheel', and never moving beyond it. It is stagnation in evolution, getting you nowhere.

This is all ended now, as Mother/Father God of this Universe has sent an edict that Earth has to move on, and can no longer hold the rest of the Galaxy back. All the other planets in your Solar System have already ascended, and it is only Earth that the whole Milky Way Galaxy has been waiting for. The laggards won't be able to hold Earth back any longer. From now on, all laggards will incarnate on an isolated planet where they won't be allowed to interfere with the evolution of a species, planet, Galaxy or Universe again. This is the edict that has been handed down from our Great Central Sun, Alpha and Omega.

Soon you will be feeling only bliss, as all negative forces and destructive entities will be leaving en masse through death, and exiting out of your Universe. The long suffering is over, and you will be free at last, and will experience life as it was always meant to be experienced. You can feel this bliss now; feel the anticipation now, and bring it into your lives now – for it is already here, and will be getting stronger and stronger each day. Each day see your world through the eyes of Love and know in your heart that this is the future for Earth. I am Mikos, always directing my Love to you.

Our Portals Lead To All Star Systems

We are all gathered around me, as we step into our library and walk toward one of our many conference rooms, which are cozy and lined with the softest, supportive couches you've ever sat on. They are ergonomically structured to allow the life force to flow down our spines as we recline on them. The colors are brilliant in tone, and form a melody around our bodies. There are many of us here in this room, as I dictate my message to you. They are holding the energy, so to speak, and flowing it toward you as you sit at your computer.

Yes, our Library is a multidimensional portal and way-station for travelers around the galaxy. Beings come here from all dimensions and universes to witness the wonders of creation, that unfold when they step into the vast portals that transport them into realms beyond their imagination. It is such a wondrous place to be, and the wonders are limitless. It takes infinity to experience them all, as life and learning go on indefinitely and forever. There is always more to learn and more places to go. This is what awaits you all when you visit us in the Hollow Earth, and are invited to enter the Library of Porthologos. It is written on your cosmic passport, that once you are here in our realm, your entry to the portals is assured. It is the opening to all of creation, and it is located right here in the center of your Earth. What a wondrous journey awaits you. We keep our doors open to all who come, and once you are here, you come with a divine ticket to enter. Your ticket of admittance is encoded in your DNA. You can also come at night, in your sleep state, for a preview of what lies ahead of you when you do enter in your physical body. This will help you acclimate to the real 'show' so that when you finally do enter our realm it will seem so familiar to you, and you'll feel that you've been here before.

There are portals leading to all Star Systems in our Milky Way Galaxy, just waiting for you to explore. You will become a Star Traveler, learning from each Star System as you make your way around the galaxy. This is a never-ending journey of course, because life goes on forever, and exploration goes on forever as our universes keep expanding exponentially into infinity. This gives us something to do. For life is about 'doing'. We need something to do in life in order to bring us the experiences for our soul growth. And the Creator supplies more universes than we could ever possibly explore in all of infinity, which just keeps unfolding and unfolding as our experiences increase. Can you imagine this? Your stepping down into our realm is the first step of your exploration out of limitation and density and into the unlimited vastness of experience and space. Our portals offer you all this and more, along with the comforts of home as you travel back and forth.

We have been here for eons, and yet have explored only a fraction of our galaxy…and there are billions of galaxies in billions of universes just waiting for us all to visit. Your life will forevermore be filled with excitement, and you'll never again find yourself saying: "what shall we do today?"

Portal to the Sun

We are attired in our finest clothing to meet with you this morning. The sun is shining overhead, and we are standing on the steps of the Library of Porthologos about to enter this vast portal, and take you inside with us. Walk with us now, as we surround your etheric body with our light and love. We usher you into our great entrance hall, that is lined in beauty and light and that sings to our souls. We will walk but a few steps to one of the moving staircases that will take us to a portal where we can witness the vastness of our galaxy. It is the galactic portal to this galaxy, and from there we can choose the destination where we desire to go. It is the fastest means of travel. No ticket or luggage is required, just our hearts intention. So here we go. We stand beside the entrance to this portal, where we form our destination desire, before entering. Are you ready? Let's go to the center of our Sun, where you have many friends and lineage waiting for you. Ok? Let's step in now, focus on the Sun, and we are there. It is that quick. See around you the brilliant light and feel the love that permeates your body and soul, and hear the choruses of angelic music. Sananda is here, and he greets you in his loving embrace and covers you with his light. We start walking now toward the community above the horizon, just a few steps away. It is nestled in hues of color and warmth and the houses are all different shades of vibrant colors. People are all outdoors, tending their fields and visiting and just lounging around. All are receptive and joyous to greet us, and knew of our intention of coming. These beings have all made their passage from Earth, and given the opportunity to live here on the Sun for as long as they like. They passed their earthly tests with flying colors, and earned this opportunity to reside here in the great love and light of our Sun, which is a planet also, but a planet of such great light that it lights your whole solar system. This is what the Earth is turning into. It is turning into a great sun star that in turn will give life and light and warmth to other planets in its solar system. And it, too, has earned this. As the Earth moves up in consciousness, she will ignite into a blazing sun star, and take all those souls who are attuned to her, with her. The other souls will be taken to another planet to continue along in their evolution, until they too, reach such states of light, that they, too, will have this opportunity to relocate into a higher frequency realm.

So our visit is about over. We now walk back to the portal and focus on returning to the Library of Porthologos, where we now again are standing on the steps. We all hug you goodbye, and thank you with the fullness of our hearts for making this journey with us today. It is indeed a grand celebration when we meet with you for these sessions. We bid you adieu.

Spaceports Inside the Earth

There are spaceports based inside Earth's interior, inside her mountains, beneath the oceans, inside the Hollow Earth cavity, that will take you on jaunts out to your solar system so you can witness first-hand the life on the planets around you. You will be in awe of Earth's majesty and in awe of God's creation – always humble and respectful as your experiences and beliefs drastically change into a knowingness that has up until now eluded you.

You are in for the thrill of your life. So just hold on as Earth goes through her changes, and know that you will be safe and cared for, no matter where your destination is. Every soul will be accounted for and every soul provided for in the great "play" called life on Earth.

It is now the ending scene, and you are about to take your bows and leave the surface stage forever. You will reappear in another grand play, only this time you will play out your parts on a more conscious level, with more control of your lines and actions and in more control of your lives.

We in the Hollow Earth will be with you this time, helping and encouraging you to reach your fully conscious state, so that the whole planet can embark together on its next leg of the journey through life.

5. Free Energy and Abundance

The Earth provides FREE Sources of ENERGY

We speak to you today on behalf of our Beloved Mother Earth, in whose womb we dwell. All our lives we have lived in peace and abundance, always knowing that all we could ever need would be provided for us. This is the responsibility of a mother. This is the purpose of our Earth – to provide abundance to all life living upon her. We have accepted all that the Earth has given to us, in gratefulness, without ever taking more than we need. All of us understand the great Universal Laws of Life, and all of us live by them. These laws are simple and logical, and state that, whatever you sow, you reap. We live our lives in harmony with our Earth Mother, and in return she supplies us with all we need. It is a quite simple law to follow, and reaps great riches.

The Earth is a self-sufficient planet, supplying all that life needs from within her own body. She is ever replenishing herself, and ever replenishing her harvests.

You are taking more from the Earth than you need, since energy is free, but you insist on using fossil fuels instead of cultivating the free sources of energy that are plentiful to everyone on the planet. This is depleting the Earth of her natural resources, which in reality function as parts of her body. When these parts are continually mined and depleted, the Earth will not be able to function. Just as if someone mined your heart center, you would not be able to survive. Every part of Earth serves a function, and must function in order for her to survive.

There's a world of free energy out there, just waiting for you to harness. There's electromagnetic energy, wind, solar, tidal and others that you haven't even discovered yet. This cold winter is giving you a great opportunity to develop other forms of fuel to heat your homes and run your industries. How fortunate prices for gas are soaring, for its purpose is to bring to your attention the availability of other energy sources that are FREE. Why pay a utility company for what the Earth provides for free?

The Earth has always given you more than you need, but in your greed you have stripped her of her resources of gold and uranium and other metals, which are her life force. Soon your people will wake up to the unlimited supply of solar and water/hydrogen power.

Use this 2001 energy crisis to develop forms of free energy and you will unburden both the Earth and yourselves.

We in the Hollow Earth never pay for anything; for all the Earth gives us is free and this freedom allows us to cultivate our creativity and spirituality and relationships which results in 'Heaven on Earth' for us.

Harmony Restores the Flow of Abundance

We've been waiting patiently for you on the steps of the Library of Porthologos, in the stillness of the Hollow Earth, where all is serene.

Today we greet you in the Light of the One Creator, the Creator of all, no matter where you live on this Earth. We were all designed by the Great Designer, and here to fulfill the divine plan for Earth.

Today we will talk about life inside the globe, and how it glorifies our existence in physical form. Everything here is in a heightened state of evolution, and everything here responds immediately to our thoughts. We command the elements, and the elements work with us, not against us, to bring us our perfect climate and perfect environment. Everything responds to everything, and together creates a synergy of resonating melodies that uplift and nourish our souls. We are constantly being fed by the vibrations of all life around us, restoring ourselves continuously and fully with the great life force necessary for our existence in immortality.

You on the surface are diametrically opposed to everything and everyone, sheltered in your own realities of separateness, and not heeding the forces of nature who are there to work with you, but whom you deem necessary to destroy and plunder. This is a great travesty of life, and as a result your environment is crashing at a rapid pace. The most important lesson to learn in this lifetime, is to live in harmony with all life, all people, all of nature. Once humanity learns this, then the great forces of abundance will flow to everyone, and suddenly everyone will have everything they could ever need. It is all available to you right now, once harmony is restored on the surface.

But you who read these messages know this, and are carrying vast amounts of Light. And it is your Light that is touching the garments of all you come in contact with and raising the vibration of the planet. It is your Light that is blazing through the density, clearing the haze of distortion so that humanity can, once again, see clearly.

6. Technology

Our Technology Advances Our Civilization
Greetings from the Hollow Earth. I am Mikos, your friend from inside the Earth. Thank you for opening your computer to talk to us. We are all gathered around me, as I dictate this message to you from underground. We are also gathered around you, in your office, as you type this dictation. We are holding the energy, and the Light of protection around you, as you sit at your computer.

Today we will talk about the technology inside the Earth. We are all technologically advanced inside the Earth, and all of our technology is used for construction, not destruction, of our civilizations. We use all our technology for only the highest purposes to advance our civilizations and improve our living conditions. We already live very well, and we are always refining our living mode, as each step upwards is another step to God. We are always advancing in everything we do, whether it is for ourselves or for others.

On the surface, your technology is used to make and amass weapons of destruction, to be used on the human race. But remember, when you use weapons of destruction on the human race, you are also eradicating the other species that share this planet with you, and you are also upsetting their habitants, leaving them homeless too. Have you ever thought about this? Your karma for destruction is great, because it is not only for humans, but the elemental kingdom and animal kingdom and the trees that you maim and obliterate when you use your weapons of mass destruction.

You have reversed the purpose for developing technology in the first place. Its purpose is to advance living conditions and create ease and plenty for everyone, not to harm and destroy each other and the land. This is a gross misuse of God's technology that was given to you to improve your lives and experiment with different ways of living, not to destroy the very lives that you were meant to improve. There is a great misunderstanding here, that we wish to clarify for you. Although most of the Earth's population is loving and yearns only for peace, there are still thousands who wish to control the population of Earth, including all her resources. They do this through war and threats.

The only way to advance is through the heart center, where love from God flows to each and every one of us. Here, in the Hollow Earth, our hearts are always open, and always receiving the love that is pouring in from God. Love is all we feel. It is this same love that is also pouring into your hearts on the surface. All you have to do is open to receive it, and you will feel its wonders in every thought you think and every emotion you feel. You will be tuned into God, even though your feet still touch the Earth.

Electrons Remain Intact In Our Water

We don't use the same technology to bring our water to us as you on the surface do. Our 'pipes' operate differently, so that when our water flows through them, the electrons remain intact. **When water flows through the pipes on the surface, the electrons spin off, resulting in the loss of life force. So you drink 'dead' water, due to the way water spirals through your pipes.** This does not occur in the Hollow Earth or Subterranean Cities, because we know how to flow water to keep its electrons intact and protect its life force. So the water we drink is alive. It is living consciousness.

When we emerge and come to the surface, we will bring our equipment with us, connected to the Hollow Earth oceans, and deliver water to you that you've never tasted before; water that invigorates your spirit, renews your cells and rebuilds your body. We will clean all your oceans and streams, and show you how to harness the life force and bring it right into your homes.

We Store Our Records On Telonium Plates

I am talking to you from my office in the Library of Porthologos, where I transcribe and prepare all ancient, current and future records for our Telonium plates. Telonium is an ancient and eternal kind of metal that lasts forever and never shows any signs of decay. It is the perfect material to store our records on. This process of storage is quite a creative one, and it's a joy to indulge ourselves in the creation process of preserving all of Earth's records, along with all the records in our Universe. It is a process of extreme creativity, not like working in a surface copy shop or the mundane repetition of factory work.

7. Uncovering Our Existence

We Are the Diamonds and You Are the Miners

We are here, embedded in the Earth's core, like sparkling diamonds buried in a mine. You can only reach us by uncovering the stratums of Earth that cover up our Light. You do this by clearing yourself of all impurities and emotional blocks, so that your vision is clear and focused. Once your sight is attuned to our frequency, you will see us clearly, sparkling under the Inner Central Sun of the inner sphere of Earth. For though you do not as yet 'see' us, you can feel our existence under you by connecting with us in consciousness. You will physically feel your vibratory rate increase, and your crown chakra will bubble and pulse. This is a physical manifestation of your connection to us.

Yes, We are the diamonds buried inside the Earth, and you are the miners about to reach down and uncover our existence below you. **Soon, we will receive the directive from the Confederation of Planets, to swing open the Tunnel Entrances for you to physically enter our realm and explore the inside cavity of Earth.**

Be assured that we will have guides leading you through the tunnels, seating you on our electromagnetic vehicles and escorting you to our cities where you will be cheered and congratulated for reaching the frequency where you can visit us at last. When this occurs, it will be the sign that the Earth's ascension is imminent. What a glorious day this will be. For not only we and you will celebrate, but the Whole Universe will be applauding your emergence out of density; signaling to all that our Whole Galaxy is now prepared to move, as a whole, to a higher octave of existence.

For remember, that **WITH UNITY CONSCIOUSNESS, WE ALL ACCELERATE AS ONE — ONE UNIVERSE ACCELERATING ON HER COURSE THROUGH ETERNITY**, through the ever-expanding Light of God, of All That Is.

The Earth herself is a diamond, a multifaceted gem radiating the brilliance of God's Eternal Light. It is only surface folk, separated by the veils of density, who are blinded to the brilliance surrounding them. The brilliance is within your souls, within the Earth, and within all life everywhere. Just turn your eyesight inwardly, feel your connection to All That Is, and your Inner World will light up and resonate to the diamond you are. Through this resonance, all of Earth will open up to you in all its glory and splendor, and you will see all and know all. For indeed, it ALL IS WITHIN YOU. The world of Light is within your soul. It is self-lit by the Source of All and sustained Eternally.

The merging of our two civilizations will signal the accomplishment of the Divine Plan on Earth, and you will be free to evolve up the Spiral of Evolution at long last, without the impediments and blockages and obstacles and density of the last 12 million years. So rise with us in consciousness, as we merge into One Diamond of Sparkling Light wrapped around and through our entire planet. I am Mikos of the Diamond Light.

The Library of Porthologos is in a Huge, Carved-Out Cavity

The Library of Porthologos is vast and round, situated within the inside of the Hollow Earth cavity. We are in a huge, carved-out cavity. We are not out in the open as you might imagine. Mother Earth keeps her inner grounds pristine by providing living space within her interior body and not out in the open spaces.

Our inner caverns are perfectly suited to our living style and when we want to swim in the oceans or climb the mountains, it is but a short trip to the center of the Hollow Earth cavity in our electromagnetic vehicles that levitate through the vast tunnel system in just minutes of your time. You will all experience this soon, as the time of our emergence will bring us to you and we will escort you to our homes within the Earth. All is lit up in the softest and clearest of light, and the temperatures are perfectly suited to our health and strength.

All our lives we've waited for this moment to connect with you on the surface, and now it is here. Our hearts are brimming over with love for all our lost brothers and sisters, and we yearn to connect to each and every one of you again. Our hearts are one.

Our Haven Underground

There are so many Catharians gathered around me, Mikos, as I dictate this message to you. We are out on the grounds that surround the great Library of Porthologos. We are sitting on grass that is as soft as a cushion, breathing in the fragrant, oxygen-filled air that keeps us eternally young and vibrant. This pure air is "nectar" to our lungs, and keeps our bodies free from disease.

The oxygen on the surface has reached such low levels that you are being oxygen starved, which opens the way for pathogens to invade your body. We, here in the Hollow Earth, breathe clean, pure air, and drink the purest of water, which is still as pure as the day Earth was created.

We are so fortunate to be living in this haven under the ground. We sit here, propped up comfortably on our pillows and stools, just breathing in the air and smelling the scents of the enormous flowers blooming all around us. This is a wonderland of beauty, and this beauty is reflected in our souls.

Our bodies respond to our environment, and out-picture what surrounds us. And what surrounds us is magnificent to behold. We are surrounded by trees and flowers that emanate strength and health, and we in turn feel this strength and health, and our bodies conform to this picture. So our bodies mirror our surroundings. They mirror the perfection of our environment. We, in turn, mirror perfection back — thus completing the cycle of perfection that is never ending. Because of this perfect cycle, our bodies can remain in a perpetual state of perfection, never sickening, nor aging, nor dying. It is a closed cycle of perfection.

It is noon here now, and we bask in the full spectrum light of our Inner Central Sun, as it hangs in our "sky." Our sky is the very center of the Hollow Globe, and our sun doesn't move, as your sun appears to. Ours just hangs there, "dead center", held by the forces of gravity pulling around its circumference so that it is perfectly balanced and remains in place.

The inside of the Earth is concave, and spirals up and across and around us. So our picture of "heaven" is from a different perspective or angle than yours. You look straight "up", and we look "around" us. So today, as always, the sun is shining down upon our gathering here on the Library Grounds. Our work here in the Library is not work as you term it, but joy to our hearts. We do what we love, and we do it in leisure. We have no time clocks to punch, and no time clocks to tell us when to stop. We each know what we want to accomplish each day, and we stay as long as we want or until we complete our work. However, we don't set long hours the way you do on the surface. Our workday is short compared to yours. In terms of hours, our workday is less than half the hours of your work day. So should we want to work "overtime", we have the flexibility of doing so without it infringing on the other areas of our lives. And our lives remain always balanced, because our schedules allow us the time to do so many other things each and every day, above and beyond the hours we spend on our "jobs".

We live perfectly balanced lives of ease and comfort, and have created everything we need to develop our talents, expand our minds, and strengthen our bodies. We have music and dance conservatories and theatres everywhere. We are always dancing and singing together, fine tuning our talents and evolving them to do more and more creative things.

Our lives are filled with creativity, and we delight in what we create. For what we create is shared with all, so that we all benefit from each other's talents and abilities. We all teach each other and we all learn from each other. We thrive on cooperation, we thrive on sharing, and we thrive on giving as much as we can to each other, which means that we end up having all that we've all created. So our gifts are multiplied — our blessings are multiplied — and we reap the abundance of our civilization underground. Nothing is hoarded or "owned", as you do on the surface, for it's not necessary, nor even logical, when you understand that we are all a part of the Earth, and therefore everything belongs to everyone, and yet nothing is owned by anyone, because everything is free for everyone to use.

Sharing is the key — not owning. Just change your words and you will change your ways. And changing the way you do things will change your lives — and will bring them back into balance, so that you, too, will have the leisure to develop your creativity and talents and explore the Earth, rather than devour her. For once you explore the intricacies and beauty and magic of Nature, you cannot abhor and destroy her, you can only emulate and love her, and know beyond a doubt that she is you, and you are her. **For whatever you destroy outside yourself, you destroy within yourself,** for Nature out-pictures you, as much as you out-picture Nature.

Just look around you at the devastation of Earth's forests and oceans, and it will show you the parts of yourself that you are destroying inside your very own bodies. The Earthquakes that are becoming so prevalent on the surface are now surfacing within your very own emotional and physical bodies.

Everything you do to the Earth, you do to yourself. Remember, there is only <u>one</u> consciousness. You and We are part of the <u>one</u> consciousness. As you destroy a part of the one, the other parts are affected.

You are not separate from the Earth. You are the Earth; you just don't know it yet. But as you wake up from your deep slumber of millions of Earth years, you will remember the connectiveness of all life, and how the health of one is connected to the health of all. Surface humans cannot survive if they destroy their surroundings and wage wars on their own species, just because they live on different parts of the planet.

We, here in Porthologos, are so grateful to each blade of grass, to each petal on a flower, to each leaf on a tree. For the harmony we feel is the same harmony that the flowers and trees feel, and which enables us to grow in stature and accounts for the enormity in size of our trees, which tower above the ground like your skyscrapers, because nothing is holding them back. They and we are free to grow in size, free to expand ourselves, because everything is in a state of expansion, not contraction as you witness and experience on the surface.

When you are "open" to life, you can only expand. When you are in struggle and lack and fear, you can only close down and diminish your stature, for fear of being seen or fear of standing out among others. You squelch your power, squelch your intuition, squelch your feelings, trying to fit into the mold of the lowest common denominator of the people around you. This stunts not only your physical growth, but your soul growth as well. When you open to the fact that you and the Universe are <u>one</u>, you will awaken to all that you are and begin to expand your horizons and literally grow in size — height and width.

Your mind and body are connected. If you think small, you grow small. If you think life only exists on Earth's surface and nowhere else, then you've shortened yourself, which shortens your physical height, just as your thoughts have shortened your vision. Expand your thoughts, and you expand your world; expand your world, and your body responds in spurts of growth and renewal.

If you only knew all that you are, you would be living like Kings and Queens, in palaces of gold, not on dirty, littered city streets. You've dethroned yourself, and you don't even know it.

Wake Up, Surface Dwellers! For if you don't, the Earthquakes within your souls will blast you back into consciousness of who you are — and that might mean the devastation of your current living conditions being turned to rubble.

Although it's hard work to dig yourself out of an earthquake, once you're free of its rubble and you see that everything you "owned" is gone, you will awaken with the shock and realize that all you have is yourself. Suddenly, from within the depths of your Being, you find the strength and wisdom that was buried inside you. Earthquakes clear density, so sight is restored and vision returned, enabling you to see and be all that you truly are.

Our vision has always been clear, since density does not cloud our vision underground. We see clear and far, because nothing obstructs our vision. We can see out among the Stars, even though we're under the ground, because nothing impedes our sight.

When you clear yourselves of all belief systems and negative thoughts and negative feelings, you too will feel the clarity and harmony within yourselves, and will be able to see all that has been kept from you by your governments. You will be able to "see through" all their deceit, and the truth about life on other planets and life within the Earth will shine through your eyes and be fully exposed to all.

We are still sitting here beneath our sun as I bring this dictation to its end. We thank you for taking our message.

8. Time, Telepathy, and Consciousness

The Amount of Time You Have in Each Day
Is Determined by Your Level of Consciousness

I am Mikos, Guardian of Earth's Records. Today we will speak about Time, the Time warp that envelops Mother Earth. Earth is out of time with the rest of the Universe, in order for her evolutions to learn the lessons of their souls. Time operates differently here on Earth's surface, for its peoples need to repeat life's lessons over and over again until they are learned and mastered. That is why you have the concept of past, present and future – to give your evolving human species the time they need to learn their lessons and pass the tests necessary for mastery. So Earth time plays an important factor in evolution.

When a planet evolves and is in the Ascended State, there is no more time, for from this higher perspective of consciousness you can see into Eternity – and can feel the oneness of all time simultaneously. You indeed experience your multidimensionality, which is experiencing all states of consciousness and all time and places at once. There are no longer any demarcations or divisions or separateness. All is ONE, and all is simultaneous.

As Earth and all life on her surface evolve in consciousness, time compresses. It becomes less and less, which is a sign that humans are evolving in consciousness. This results in less and less time, until you reach the point in your consciousness when you're no longer "in" time – you've moved out of it into the Ascended State.

As you move higher and higher in your awareness of your self and all of Earth, you will find that the days speed by, even the minutes and hours fly by, and before you know it, morning turns into night before you've accomplished even half of what you used to be able to accomplish.

Time is actually becoming elusive. You can't hold onto it any longer. The denser an evolution is, the more time there is, and the days appear longer. The higher the vibration of a species, the shorter the day appears, as they are actually connecting with "Cosmic Consciousness", which is a state of multidimensionality where "no time" exists. Everything just "is".

As time further collapses, you will move into the multidimensionality that you are, and experience "All That Is" profoundly. You will see and feel the Oneness of all Creation, and how all life is intertwined and interconnected. This is what humanity is here to learn. But up until now Earth's density has been so thick that each person has felt separated and alone, and cut off from others. Each person has felt separated by time and space – which in actuality does not exist. It only exists on "evolving" planets so that its species does not get sidetracked and can focus in on what it came here to do.

Time flow has nothing to do with age. It does not speed up when you are older. It only speeds up when you are wiser and have "grown" in consciousness and wisdom. Therefore, if you equate age with wisdom and illumination, then indeed you could say that as you age, time speeds up. But for those who don't evolve in consciousness during their life spans, then time seems interminably long and drawn out for them. They could say that "time gets slower" as they get older. So you see, it's your own perspective, your own rate of evolution that determines times length – and determines the length of each of your own days. You all have different day lengths and different amounts of time, determined by your state of consciousness. So as your consciousness expands, your minutes and hours decrease in reverse ratio; until you're no longer in a time zone, but in an Ascended State of Enlightenment, where there's no time, no space – only the Oneness of all Creation.

This is what we experience in the Hollow Earth. We feel the ONENESS and ETERNITY of existence. And this Oneness and Eternity is what you are beginning to experience on the surface, in small increments, as the Light of the Creator is pouring onto Earth and causing your consciousness to expand with the illumination of God's Light.

We don't feel the "crunch" of time, as you would say. We feel only the Eternal flow of life ebbing through us, which brings us peace and contentment in every "moment" of our day. We <u>don't</u> even have clocks (as you do and rely upon). We count time in a much different, cosmic way, that's in synchronicity with the whole cosmos. Because we are part of the cosmos, and function as part of the cosmos, we are on "cosmic time" – which is much different from surface time.

As the Light is rapidly illuminating the Earth, soon your consciousness will reach into cosmic time, and you will find us waiting for you there, which is right here – in the NOW. We wish you a speedy journey in consciousness.

You Have More Than Five Senses

This is Mikos, speaking to you today from the Hollow Earth. We come here to meet with you to give you messages to take to your people who are above ground. It is so very important that the people here on Earth know who we are and that we are here. Our existence is crucial to your existence. You are much wiser now as a species and will more easily accept us when we physically contact you now.

This Hollow Globe you live above was meant for all to partake in, was meant for all to explore, was meant for all to realize how magnificent the God within is. For it is the God within your being who has created all of this, and it is the God within your being who wants to experience all of this. But first you have to recognize its existence and recognize that things do exist beyond your five senses, beyond that which you call sight and sound and location, for **you don't need to be able to see something in order for it to exist. Its existence is independent of your actual physical sight.**

In actuality, you will have many more than the five senses. In actuality, you are all multidimensional beings, who are here to discover the other senses within your multidimensionality. And when you discover your extra senses, you will discover the Universe. You won't need books to learn from anymore, for all of the learning will take place within you. You'll be able to travel any place you desire, and learn from the actual experience of going there. Books will become obsolete, for the real place of knowledge is within. As Jesus said, know yourself, and you will know everything. For _you_ are the source of everything, _you_ are where everything is stored; you only need to learn _how_ to access the Living Library within your very being, within your very body, within your Temple.

Marvelous things await you as you raise yourself in consciousness and raise yourselves to higher frequencies of Light Vibrations. The higher you vibrate, the more you can access, and the more you can access, the more of yourself you will know. All knowledge is within you, and you are within all, and it is quite simple to access it once you've moved up your vibration to the necessary frequency where suddenly all becomes available to you and all becomes a gift from the Grand Creator of All That Is.

So the purpose of life is to move up in vibration, until you are where we are, until all you can see is pure essence of life, the pure essence of all that is, and this pure essence is the Nirvana that you all have been looking for. The pure essence of God, which dwells in each of us, is the essence that creates the Worlds Within the Worlds.

You are now reaching the point in your evolution where it will be very easy for you to access all that is, to access the greatness of your body cells, and once again unite with us in consciousness. And once this uniting takes place, you will greatly benefit from all that we have learned over these eons of time. For we have been able to put our consciousness to work, so to speak, to create a Nirvana inside the Globe of Mother Earth.

Mother Earth knows of the existence of all of her children; she knows where each of us is, how each of us is, and where we're all going on our path to destiny. As you raise yourself in consciousness, you will also be able to check in with Mother Earth and she will tell you how you're doing as your consciousness registers within her, as the Light of your being is known by her, as all that you do and all that you say is heard by her. So you are, indeed, fully equipped to begin your journey into the bright light of a new Earth, into the bright light of the new world, where we all excitedly await your return.

There Is No Delay in Telepathic Transmissions

All are standing around me as I relay this dictated message to you that you are receiving hundreds of miles above us. For thought pierces directly through the Earth, and you receive this thought at the same time that I, Mikos, am thinking it.

There is no delay in telepathic transmissions. You hear what I say instantaneously, at the exact moment that I say it. It is quite a miraculous way to communicate, and also quite a natural way, as you will soon all realize as you raise yourself in harmony with us; for it is in this harmonious mode that telepathic communication can take place. For it is the harmony of our beings that meld and merge into one another so that we can talk to each other whenever we so desire.

Open yourselves up to the existence of other life existing beside you on your home planet and you will be able to explore all the wonders that truly do exist inside this globe you call Earth. She is a wonder in herself, our Earth, and the more you come to know her, the more you come to know yourself and the more you come to know all life. For the existence of all life can be accessed by you as you move yourself up into higher frequencies of consciousness. We can see and hear all of you who live above us, as you are all very closely monitored by us. We know of all that takes place on the surface through our vision and through our computer system, where all on Earth is monitored closely and where our emissaries come in and out of our habitat, bringing us news and also relaying information to surface dwellers.

Our emissaries are in contact with many surface dwellers who work with us in the dissemination of information regarding the conditions on the surface. We do have quite a system going that will greatly surprise you. Until that time approaches when you will be able to visit, I will be speaking directly to you, exchanging information with you from the Hollow Earth that you can access within your very own beings.

So do connect with us in consciousness, as we are all here and all very eager to return your reply. **We will speak to all who consciously connect with us in sincerity of heart,** for it is our greatest wish to connect with you and help you through these times where you will soon be aware of all life on Earth and where we all will recognize all of us as ONE. I am Mikos, and I bid you good day.

Telepathy

You have been gifted beyond measure with talents and intelligence that are now surfacing. Many of you are regaining your gifts that were hidden from your sight. One of these is telepathy.

You are all telepathic, and you can all converse with Us. You are just now beginning to realize how gifted humans really are. So gifted, that in fact you could actually do everything that we do, because we were once you.

We once went through all that you are now experiencing. But with our entry into the cavity of Earth, we were destined to evolve, just as you are destined to evolve as the Earth's frequency speeds up. Your innate gifts will shine through and you will rejoice at your capabilities. Once you reach a certain frequency, your consciousness will burst through the density and you will see all and know all, and we will be here with you at last, enfolding you in our love.

You Are the Knower of All

You are the knower of ALL
You are the receiver of ALL

You are the ONE component necessary for ALL to exist
Your existence is the primary factor
for the existence of the Universe
Without you, each and every one of you
there could be no life
You are all an integral part in the design
and not one of you is superfluous

Know how important you are
Know how necessary you each are
For without each one of you, there is nothing

Your existence makes up the substance of ALL THAT IS
You are each the necessary ingredient
That makes the Universe work with precision

9. Cures for Pollution and Diseases

Once Your Pollution is Cleared Up
Your Diseases Will Vanish

We have the answers to all your pollution problems that your greedy politicians and secret governments have created. And once we have surfaced, we will put our technologies into operation to solve all your pollution problems and all your health problems. Once your pollution is cleared up, your diseases will vanish. For your diseases are only caused by you polluting your air, water and foods. It's so simple, if you would but grasp the truth of it.

Here in the Hollow Earth, we never pollute anything, as this word does not even exist for us. We live in complete harmony with our surroundings and our people know that we are all a part of each other. We would never do anything to harm one another, nor would the thought ever cross our minds. We feel only love for each other, and love for our surroundings and love for our Mother Earth. It is this love component that you are missing on the surface. You've put everything before love, and lost your sight and lost your way. It is now time to return love back into your lives, and it will solve all your surface problems in the quick of a wink.

We follow your thoughts from below, and send our love to intercept your thoughts from above, hoping to gently guide you into a state of pure love in your thinking process. For when your thoughts become the beacons of pure love radiating out from you, you will bring the peace and harmony to your surface civilizations that you all desire so much.

I am Mikos, radiating my love to you all the time. Bon Jour, my traveling companions above.

The Cure For All Diseases Already Exists

Today is a celebration for Us in the Hollow Earth. We are celebrating our climb into Light, for we've reached a demarcation, a certain level of growth that we have been working toward for some time now. It's a whole new way of looking at life; it's reaching another step on the ladder of evolution and it's an exciting time for us as we embark on experiencing this whole new perspective to life. Each level we reach is an eye-opener, and we wonder how we couldn't have seen this before. This is similar to your eye openers on the surface, as it is the way all life evolves. More and more of the 'unseen' becomes the 'seen'.

This is now happening to you also on the surface. More and more is being revealed to you on your newscasts and newspaper. This is an exciting time for you too, for that which is being revealed has already been known for decades, but kept hidden from the public. With all the light reaching the Earth, the secrets are being exposed because Light exposes everything. It is only darkness that "covers up." You are in for the 'ride of your life', as everything that has been kept from you will suddenly come out in the media. What a 'shake up' will soon occur.

The medical groups, corporations and governments that have been covering up the cures to diseases and then spending billions of your tax dollars to 'find' cures, will be exposed. These groups caused the diseases in the first place, and could have easily stopped them years ago. Instead, they've used disease as a profit generator – a way to make billions of dollars at the expense of a suffering humanity. All the diseases have been caused by corporations and governments polluting your air, water and food with chemicals, herbicides, pesticides, fertilizers, biological germs, and you name it; along with destroying the rainforests and cetaceans. All they have to do is stop this pollution to rid the Earth of its effects. But it's their greed, at the expense of humanity and Earth that has prevailed. For they will all be exposed for exactly who they are: profiteers in the worse sense, whose goal has been to rape and destroy a planet and its people.

We have no diseases in the Hollow Earth because we grow everything organically, and know and revere the connection between our Earth and our lives. We know we are part of the Earth and whatever we do to her we do to ourselves. As more and more of humanity reconnect themselves to Nature, they will understand how to eliminate all diseases and destruction on Earth.

This is what Light does. It opens your eyes and reconnects you to the Source of all Creation, so you can again live your lives in peace and plenty and perfect health.

So join us in consciousness, as we gently lead you to Nirvana, where you will dwell with us at last.

Protect your Newborn from Inoculations

There's a whole new Earth being birthed, and all souls are now being born with telepathy and clairvoyance and great wisdom. This is why your government has its inoculation system in place in your hospitals. These inoculations jam the high frequencies of the newborn and prevent their accessing the divine gifts that they are innately endowed with. This is the purpose of these 'mandatory' inoculations – they are to keep the Light of your newborn off the planet.

So remember dear ones, not to give into the fear of your hospitals or your media, and stand in your own Light of Wisdom, of knowing that nothing can harm your newborn, as they are divinely endowed and protected from the illnesses of this planet. They come fully equipped to withstand all adverse conditions and nothing administered to them by your hospitals or doctors can protect them – it will only deflect their health from them. So protect your newborns by knowing that they are already protected from within their own DNA, and no outside antidote or inoculation can benefit them in any way.

They, too, are the Angels incarnating on Earth and being born to you at this time to bring more and more Light to Earth. As Earth's frequency of Light increases, we cheer from below, knowing that our emergence is indeed imminent. We leave now in the Light and Love of our Creator.

A Great Dispensation Has Just Been Granted

Greetings from the Library of Porthologos inside the Earth's interior. We come today to talk about the Angels *on* Earth and their work with humanity. These are great Beings of Light from many Star Systems that are visiting your Earth, and staying to help bring in the great waves of Light that are descending onto your planet. These Beings are most known to you as Angels – God's helpers in the evolution of mankind. These Beings sweep your planet with their light and wisdom, encapsulate the dark spots until the darkness fades back into Light again. The Angels are the bringers of all that is good, and they are here. And you, our dear Lightworkers, are these Angels. You are these great Beings who have come from afar, to help Earth and humanity, and now it is your turn to be helped. **A great dispensation has just been granted to all the Lightworkers on Earth, allowing the Host of Heaven to intervene to completely and totally heal your physical bodies,** so that you can withstand the coming climatic and Earth changes looming on the horizon of your planet. You have all called for help, you are always calling for the healing of your bodies, and now this help has been granted.

In a magnificent turn of events, this dispensation was unanimously approved by the whole company of heaven, and Mother/Father God of this Universe, in gratefulness for the dedication and sacrifice of all the Lightworkers on Earth – and it is time. Time to heal all aspects of yourself and time to manifest your physical strength, health, mental acuity and emotional balance. This is the gift of Heaven to its "Ground Crew". As the days and weeks go on, you will find yourself getting stronger and stronger, and all the old pains falling by the wayside. You will see and feel events clearer and clearer and come more into focus with the unseen world around you. This is truly an unprecedented gift, and it is yours.

Now, dear Lightworkers, live each day fully, in the presence of the 'now', and know that tomorrow is in God's hands, and have nothing to fear, for the Divine Plan is already accomplished and this is just the last 'play-off' of the game. All is being readied for the great 'lift-off' into higher realms of light that are waiting your entry. You have much to look forward to as you leave your old world behind and enter the new. So gird yourself with the steel of your determination and know that all that is of the Light has a glorious future and it is just a breath away – just waiting for the next deep in-breath from God.

Here in the Library of Porthologos, we have always maintained our health, strength and youthfulness inside the protective cover of the Earth's mantle. You, too, will soon be able to accomplish the same physical feats and will have the same endurance as we. For we don't get tired or sick or angry or worried, and neither, now, shall you. For these qualities are not of life – they are of illusion and mis-creation and darkness – and are not part of a life supporting system.

Your current system does not support life; hence you have sickness, fear and death. It has been decreed that these systems can no longer exist, and will be confined and quarantined like a sick patient, in a separate room. Only this time, all the sick patients will be in a ward by themselves, so they don't infect the others. No one again will have to suffer from their control and destructive contamination.

10. Evolution is the Solution, 9-11-2001

911 was Emergency Call for Help

Now we will talk about the World Trade Center and the atrocities of 9-11-2001. As you can see, 911 is the emergency number for help. On this date was a call for help from the people of the world against all terrorists. This emergency call was a shout to heaven, and all in our galaxy and beyond heard your cries for help. It was a grand unification of souls, unified in your distress and pain, and calling to God for help and for freedom from tyranny.

Your people are united on the soul level, each one wanting peace to be able to live out your life in freedom. There was a great divine response to the tragedy. This was not a set back for the Light, but instead, a grand opening for us to become part of your conscious life and to intervene even more in the affairs of Earth to bring the peace you all strive for.

Out of every tragedy comes a grand awakening, and millions more have awakened to the Light as a result of this. The dark forces are actually working for us when they scheme to perpetrate such heinous acts of violence. It wakes people from their comfort zones of slumber and they start calling on God at last and reconnect their phone line to the Divine Creator of ALL.

So look at this as another step that humanity has taken towards the Light that reaches you all from heaven. For once humanity connects again to the Light, it will flow forth to the Earth like a waterfall rushes to the ground, bathing all and soaking you through to your core with Light. It is an immersion into Light – just as Jesus baptized souls by immersing them in water – this has the same effect.

Pray for Peace. It is only through your prayers that we can intervene more fully to bring our whole planet into the Light. We pray along with you. We are part of you. We are one soul divided by the different strata of Earth, but all living the same life. Whatever happens to one, happens to us all, only on levels you are just now comprehending.

It is Fall now on your surface, and all is dying for the Earth is gearing for her rebirth into Light. Just as the Fall changes to Winter, and Winter to Spring, your hearts are going through a rebirthing process that is carrying you speedily into the photon belt of Light. You will be ready for the merger and will rejoice at the impact when suddenly you find yourself illuminated and seeing the world around you through the eyes of God. It will be a speedy delivery into Light – and, yes, you will find us there, waiting for you as we always have.

World Trade Center Inner Planes Electoral Vote

Today the Earth is relatively quiet as humanity contemplates the events of the past week. Although this was a heinous act and atrocity against mankind, it was not accidental. Those ones who chose to be there at that time had already chosen to leave the Earth and continue their ascension from the other side of the veil. They just left sooner than they normally would have – but not that much sooner. No one is caught in a catastrophe who has not chosen it on their subconscious level. Remember that there are no accidents – regardless of the magnitude of the incident – and this is no exception.

Now we will speak of the brother and sisterhood that prevail in the wake of this tragedy. This tragedy had welded people together – communities all over the Earth – in an embrace of love and unity and brotherhood. It has closed the gap of separation between peoples, showing that you are all involved in the same struggle of life and death, and showing that you are all one in the face of calamity, that you all share the same feelings and same hopes, and mainly that you all share the same prayers for your lost ones. This sameness is a big factor that has melded large groups of people together in a way that your past complacency could not.

We implore you to keep vigilant and to know beyond a doubt that the God you pray to hears every thought, every word, every gesture – and knows that the majority of people on Earth call for peace and justice in their hearts. And we mean justice – not vengeance nor retaliation – but justice heretofore not known in these past centuries.

These events of the past week have not hindered Earth's or humanity's ascension plan, but rather, have unified humanity to such an extent that in actuality the ascension has been furthered and heightened and quickened – although you who live in 3rd dimensional bodies cannot as yet fathom this. But soon you will see how this has enabled the ascension to go forth even more quickly, as the waves have snapped up even more and more people as a result of their abrupt awakening in the face of this immense tragedy and loss of lives.

Remember that God's Light never fails and that the Divine Plan for Earth is more intact than ever, and, more than ever, is now the time for all the Lightworkers to trust in the Divine Plan for the ascension of Earth and humanity. For the Light never gives up nor relinquishes its position. It may recede a bit, then comes back mightier in force and mightier in its resolve to move humanity up the scale of evolution to where these tragedies no longer can occur.

So you see, all is well on Earth and all is going according to Divine Plan. And what seems like a setback is really a speeding up of your ascension if you look deeper into the overall picture.

This has resulted in a vast awakening and a reversal that dark forces had not anticipated. These terrorist tragedies do not fragment people. Rather, they unify them in their resolve to find peace on Earth. The hell that the darkness wants to promote lies inside those individuals who perpetrate these events, and as long as people do not buy into that reality of darkness, then peace and Heaven on Earth will prevail. Even though many millions of American people want revenge, no one wants war on American soil, and deep down in people's heart spaces, all cry for peace on Earth and justice to prevail. In fact, all humanity that is constructive to life – and this is the vast majority of people on Earth – all want peace and love to prevail.

This is the call we all hear under the Earth and in the higher dimensions. The call for peace is so loud that it deafens everything else out. These calls are speeding up the ascension plan as nothing else could have, because when angry people call for revenge, they are exhibiting their hurts and scars from their past, but when interviewed on the Inner Planes at night, they all, with very few exceptions, choose peace.

So this is the vote we go by – **the Inner Planes Electoral Vote** – where all vote for peace without ballot tampering. It is the true vote and only vote that prevails. So rest assured that all is going according to Divine Will and that humanity will, indeed, ascend even sooner now.

You are the showcase of the Universe and you are surmounting and surpassing all obstacles being put in your way, and there will be more to come. For the dark is not done nor have they, as yet, given up. They will strike again, trying to thwart your passage into Light. But they will fail, as the resolve of the Lightworkers is too great and humanity is responding to the Light, not the dark.

Know that your world is safe. This drama will play itself out until there are only the "light" players left, as all the dark players will have vacated the premises and exited the stage. Their darkness will be gone and only the Light will prevail. Know that our hearts are filled with love for humanity, and as we watch the scenario from below, we feel your sadness and hear your calls for peace. We join our hearts with yours, magnifying your voices for peace on Earth. Our foresight protects us underground, for we do not act without weighing the outcome of our actions or without seeing the possible future consequences. Some day you will have this foresight, this vision to see the future based on your choices <u>before</u> you make them. Always opt for peace and love, and your future will always bring it to you. What you choose is what you get.

So we down in the Hollow Earth give you our strength and stand with you in your resolve to bring all humanity into the Light so that we, as one planet united in the Love of God, can finally ascend as a whole and move on to our destiny of Galactic Unity and Galactic Ascension for the whole galaxy.

We Monitor the Milky Way Galaxy

Pay no heed to the outbursts of negativity and hostile warfare – they are like a naughty child, just having an outburst that soon subsides into calmness and peace.

We in the Hollow Earth monitor your whole Earth and the whole Milky Way Galaxy. We have our amino-based computers that show us everything that is happening everywhere in our Galaxy and Universe and, of course, on Earth's surface. This is one of our "jobs," to keep track of everything simultaneously, and to plug the Confederation of Planets into the trouble spots on Earth as they occur.

Another war on Earth must not be tolerated. This is the end times – the end of war, the end of hate, negativity, anger, jealousy, competition, and fear.

Sleeping Giants of Yore
We speak to you from the fabled Library of Porthologos inside the Earth, but a step away from you in consciousness. You reach us by stepping down in your thoughts and, extending yourself and your imagination into our library, looking around, and "seeing" us. We stand there waiting for your entry.

Today we will talk about the Sleeping Giants from your folklore. These giants are Beings from the Hollow Earth who took residence on the surface thousands of years ago. In your folklore, you speak of them as sleeping for hundreds of years, and then awakening to find themselves in another time zone. Yes, they traveled from inside the Earth and lived on your surface for hundreds and thousands of years, studying humanity's surface population and then returning inside to report their findings. They did grow long beards, and many stories were written about them and their Herculean feats on the surface.

Know that Earth is populated with many different Beings from many different star systems, all here for the same purpose – to grow and evolve in consciousness, and to understand how humans evolve. The surface is a testing ground and experimenting station for growth and evolvement. The first four letters in "evolvement" are "love" spelled backwards. It is through love that you evolve. It is so simple – and yet it still eludes so many surface dwellers. Love is the glue – and it is through you, each and every one of you, that your world moves into higher states of consciousness, and it's all through love – love of yourself and love for your "other" selves. As you all come together in greater harmony and unity, you will feel yourselves and your reality shifting into higher vibrations of love and peacefulness, and you will gingerly step into the higher dimensions where you will begin to feel and see us. We are in these higher dimensions. For even as we reside "below" you, we are beside you. This is how "oneness" manifests.

Your world is rapidly changing and waking up, due in large part to the shock of the World Trade Center attack on September 11, 2001. This was a world emergency wake-up call, perpetrated by the dark forces in an attempt to wake you up to their presence. They have delved so deep into darkness that they have gone full circle and are now circling back into Light, and their terror is shocking people into their wake-up zone, affecting them in a polarity opposite of the dark's intention. The sleeping masses are finally being shocked into awakening to who they are – like the Sleeping Giants of yore.

You are all the Sleeping Giants who came to Earth's surface and fell into a great sleep – and who are finally awakening to what is being perpetrated on the surface. You've been caught in a great lie, believing everything the newspapers and media tell you, and never questioning the news source from whence it comes. Well, it all comes from the same one source – your government-controlled media – one viewpoint, theirs, which they program into your belief system.

As people awaken from their deep slumber of the ages, they begin to question and this is the awakening period. Soon you will all jump out of your beds and stand free with us in the higher realms of consciousness. Your Cetacean brothers and sisters wait for you there, too.

We have great monitors in the Library of Porthologos where we view surface conditions and follow your earthly lives. Nothing surprises us anymore, as we've seen it all, history repeating itself over and over again. But now we see something different – through the repetition of events – we see humanity waking up and remembering that there's more than war and strife and struggle and lack and limitation. They are remembering the Divine within them and this remembrance is the awakening. **REMEMBER AND AWAKEN.**

Once a critical mass of people is awakened, you will all float into higher consciousness instantly and the past will be a dream. We wait for you at the gates of your consciousness, and as the floodgates open, the waves of Light will carry you through. As Lightworkers, you have all prepared for this for eons, and now it is here.

The European Euro 12-31-2001

We transmit to you directly from the Library of Porthologos, where many of us spend most of our time. Although our time frame differs from yours, we still tell time and arrange our schedules and days.

The Hollow Earth is rejoicing at the magnitude of the rise in Earth's consciousness as witnessed by the announcement of the Euro on today's news, bringing many European countries together as ONE. This is a great step for the surface population, leading to a United Earth World.

We in the Hollow Earth have one system for all of us, which keeps us unified in all areas of commerce and life. It is a big step taken, and many more countries will follow.

Confusion and Turmoil on the Surface

Your health is linked to your wealth. By this we mean your emotional health – your feeling body – for the healthier you "feel," the clearer and purer your thoughts and feelings, the clearer your intentions will be. It is your intent that goes out into the Universal Fields of Light, and brings you back what you send out for. Every thought is a call, and every call has an answer. So attune yourselves to your thoughts and your feelings, and monitor what you are sending out. If you send out only what is positive, that is what you will receive.

This is a time of great confusion and turmoil on the surface, as people are being awakened by the string of events unfolding. Stay within your own center, go deep down, and feel only the calmness and tranquility that exists within you, and radiate this out to counteract the negativity and upheaval that is going on around you. This is your purpose; this is what it means to "Hold the Light." It means you are holding the Light that ever exists within you, and choosing to reflect only the light, and not the confusion around you. So go within, and stay within, even as you are existing in all outward appearances. It is so simple, yet so profound.

In the Hollow Earth, we all live from our heart center and radiate only the tranquility within us. This tranquility permeates the whole cavity of the Earth and brings us the health and riches that surround us always. As surface folk begin to live from within their heart center, this purity and strength and peacefulness will permeate your physical bodies and surface conditions, and gently bring you the peace that abides within us and inside our Earth. This is our dream for you – and OUR DREAMS ALWAYS COME TRUE.

PEACE is the Answer

We bring you tidings from the Hollow Earth located in the innermost cavity of your planet. We dwell here in peace and prosperity and great abundance. We wear precious gems and gold that adorn our bodies and homes, and everyone has as many as they could ever want. Everything is in prolific abundance – including peace and unconditional love. For it is this peace and love that creates abundance and prosperity and longevity of life. This is the secret – the magic to life.

Just live in peace and harmony and love with one another, and heaven on Earth is yours. It is truly magic. For peaceful living can only bring more peace and great riches beyond your 3rd dimensional imagination. Peace is the answer to all your societal ills. Love is the answer to all your family and relationship problems. Peace is the answer to your economic woes and stock market fluctuations. Peaceful co-existing is the purpose of life and the reason you are here. Don't let it elude you, and don't let 9/11 and other tragedies detract you from feeling peace within yourself. These events are but ploys to detract you from the peace that already exists within each of you. These events are purposely orchestrated to push humanity off the course of your impending ascension. **No matter what transpires on your surface world, stay calm and centered within your soul and "feel peace." It is only through the feelings that peacefulness can emerge.** Hold this peacefulness and let it extend out onto your surface, and touch every soul you come in contact with. This is how you spread peace and counteract the darkness around your Earth.

The Forces of Light are here in great numbers surrounding your Earth and every man, woman and child. Our Central Sun has sent Legions of Angels to guide and protect you, as the energies coming to Earth are so powerful now that everything not of Love is being pushed to the surface for healing.

We in the Hollow Earth are insulated from the chaos above, for the Earth is a great insulator and provides a protective shield all around us. We can be in contact with you, but cannot be contacted by negativity. It just can't reach us. Our shield of protection is just too strong. We've woven a force field around us that is impenetrable to everything that is not of the Light. We are secure and safe inside the Earth for it is the only way we can exist and evolve.

When you achieve these peaceful living conditions, we can then emerge and welcome you into the Confederation of Planets, where you will be shown how to change your world back into Paradise.

11. Our Immortality

We Don't Age

We have waited all day in joy, knowing that we would make our connection today, at the end of your day. We are joyous to be here with you today, partnering with you to bring our messages to our brothers and sisters above ground. Thank you for keeping your appointment with us.

Today we will speak about time and how fleeting it is on the surface. You count your days, your minutes, your seconds, and register them all in your bodies, thinking that aging signifies the passage of time. As people age, time passes. As buildings deteriorate, time passes. This is time on the surface, and it is all an illusion. Time really does not exist – it can't exist – and we are a prime example. Our bodies don't age and our buildings don't deteriorate. So does this mean that there's no time in the Inner Earth, but only time on the surface? You would think so, wouldn't you? But our lives attest to the fact that through your passage of time, our bodies stay young, no matter how much time passes on the surface. You measure your time with aging, but we don't age. Does this mean 'time stands still' for us? Or does it rather mean that you're using an inappropriate measurement?

Your bodies wouldn't age if you didn't count the days and years as 'getting older'. If you counted the days and years as your journeys around the sun, instead of 'aging', then 30 years would mean 30 trips around the sun, instead of 30 years 'old'. 'Trips' don't age you, but 'years old' does. If you just change the words from 'years old' to 'trips', you gain your immortality. It's all in your beliefs and your speech. Your speech and your thoughts make it so.

In the Hollow Earth we know there's no such thing as aging, because we never see it. We know there's no such thing as time as you experience it, because here everything is in a perpetual state of 'youthfulness' and 'newness'. Everything looks as new as the day it was created, including our bodies. We exist in a state of divine perfection, in an environment of 'timelessness'.

We never 'hurry' and are never 'late', and we never 'kill time' as you do on the surface. Have you noticed how this is a favorite saying of yours? It's as if time were your enemy, and whenever you have some <u>extra</u> time you 'kill it'. You are in a rush to use up all the time in your life, so that the end comes fast, and you don't have to 'feel'. You just stay busy, watch the years of your life pass, and hope it ends without leaving any 'extra' time on your hands. For what would you do with 'extra' time? The thought would scare you, for it would leave you time to <u>feel</u> yourself, to <u>feel</u> your life, and <u>feeling</u> is what everyone wants to avoid. So without enough time left at the end of each day, you can avoid 'feeling' and just continue a robot-like existence.

You can stop time. Just start feeling yourself in every moment and prolong this feeling, this consciousness of yourself. You can actually expand your 'time', and prolong your youthfulness, by not getting caught up in 'time'. If it starts slipping away from you, you can stop to recapture it by feeling yourself deeply in the moment. It's all about awareness. If you lose yourself in your day, you lose a segment of your life. If you're aware of yourself throughout your day, you gain immortality; for you're focusing on the 'now'.

You would love our easy life style and slow, harmonious ways. We have 'time' to think things out, to talk things out, before we make choices. We're never forced to choose because 'time is running out' or there's a 'deadline'. These are obstacles that you've created on the surface, and they just don't exist 'down here'.

We thank you for taking your 'time' today to meet with Us. I am Mikos, ageless and timeless.

We Have The Eyes Of Falcons

Today it is bright and glorious inside the Hollow Earth, as our Inner Sun is always shining and there are never any clouds in our sky. Our vision is always clear, and we can see for miles around our inner cities, and across our sky to the other side of our inner earth. We have the eyes of falcons, with intense, precise vision. No one here wears glasses, as our sight is perfect. Seeing is believing, and soon you will be able to see us with your inner vision, and wonder how you had never seen us before. As your consciousness climbs in frequency, so does the perfection of your body expand to every cell and organ, until you return to the divine perfection that you are.

Frequently Asked Questions of Hollow Earth Inhabitants

Q: Will you give us a physical description of yourself?
A: Yes, my eyes gleam with crystal light and my skin is soft as a baby. I am 15 feet tall, and hefty and stronger than an ox. I can jump across streams and wade through rivers and climb the highest mountains, all without tiring. I am in perfect condition, although I am over 483,000 years old – and I remain in divine perfection as we all do here in the Hollow Earth. No thought forms exist here that are less than divine, so all we think we become. It is the Law of Life. You, too, are realizing this on the surface. Hence you witness the upsurge of your transformational workshops taking place where you

are taught that all you believe you create. It is a simple law of life. I am Mikos.

Q: What kind of clothes do you wear?
A: We are all gathered together, here on the grass of the Library of Porthologos. We love to work outdoors, and take every opportunity to do so. We are very casual in our attire, and dress comfortably throughout the day. We have no set rules for dress codes, as you on the surface do. We dress according to how we feel - and we always feel good. So we dress in loose, brightly colored soft fabric clothing, made from hemp and other vegetable materials. We never use trees for anything, as they are Living Beings here to adorn our landscape, give us oxygen to breathe and serve as a home to other species.

Q: Do you have streets?
A: We don't have streets. We have paths lined with flowers and composed of earth, so that our feet are always 'grounded', and we often walk barefooted as our earth is 'clean' and 'pure' and massages our feet as we walk. It is the same feeling as your walking on your sandy beaches. Our feet are strong and healthy as a result, and our feet are not cramped from the constriction of shoes as yours are.

Q: Where does your Light come from?
A: The Center of the Earth is a place exquisite in beauty and unique in charm and just dazzling with the Light of our people, for they mirror the face of God in all of God's perfection. Our forms are perfect in proportion, and luminous with Light pouring out of all our cells. We don't need artificial lighting, as our very own cells provide all the light we need. Our Light, plus our Inner Sun, lights up our Inner World perfectly – and of course it's all free – with no electricity bills to pay. We generate all our own electricity and light, for we are each power generators of energy, and

supply all we need in terms of light and heat for our homes and workplaces. Of course, we have help from our crystals. Crystals, coupled with electromagnetism, generate all the power we need to meet our needs.

Q: What are your beds made of?
A: Our beds are cushioned with a vibrant material that molds perfectly to our forms, yet gives our bodies the perfect support and comfort we need to leave us fully rejuvenated upon awakening.

Q: What kind of water do you drink?
A: Our water system is pristine pure, and is living, crystallized water, with its consciousness fully intact – not like your dead water on the surface, that's devoid of life giving energy.

Q: How old are your trees?
A: Our trees are thousands upon thousands of years old, and adorn our landscapes in their majestic gowns of green. We are in full communication with all the trees, bushes, plants and flowers, and can hear their choruses and arias wafting through the air as they serenade our inner homeland.

12. Our Oceans and Beaches

Our Water is Alive with Consciousness

Good morning. It is Mikos calling to you from the ocean shore in the Hollow Earth, where I am walking along the beach watching the waves lap the sand. Our oceans are large, nay huge in comparison to yours, with waves larger in size and stronger in force. The oceans flow swiftly around our inner globe, and ebb and flow in tides affected by the Earth's outer moon just as your tides are. For the magnetic pull of the moon is felt inside the Earth as well.

We all spend much of our time on the beaches, walking on the sand along the shore, and swimming in the ocean's clean, clear water. The water in our oceans and rivers is composed of living consciousness, and it is our water's consciousness that keeps us young forever.

Your water is the elixir of life, and in its pure state it can change your bodies and actually bring the dead back to life. It can bring the life force back into each and every cell, thereby increasing the flow of consciousness in your whole body and bringing full consciousness back into every living cell. This quickening can move you beyond all earthly sicknesses and diseases, and give you the physical perfection and physical immortality you all yearn for. So drink your water 'consciously', and know that soon our pure water will arrive on the surface to cure all the ills of your people and bring them back into a higher state of consciousness.

There are already some bodies of water on the surface that are known for their curative effects, and people by the millions go to them. Soon all your bodies of water will have these curative effects and more, as we prepare ourselves to emerge from below ground and merge with you on the surface. Your bodies yearn to be freed from the distortion of sickness and disease, and yearn to feel the illumination of God's Light from within. Our water will dissolve all negativity and blockages and bacteria, so that your cells are clear to radiate the Light from God that is always flowing through you.

Your Inner Heart's Flame is always ablaze with God's Light, but the current density of the cells quench the Light's illuminating effect and instead of the Light blazing forth like a golden sun, its rays become splintered and distorted and stuck. Water and Light are necessary for life, and your cells need to be purified to hold the great Light that is emanating from your Heart's Flame, which is a true and actual flame that is lit inside your heart and composed of the consciousness of the Creator flowing through you.

So know that as the pollution of the surface has intensified, so has the pollution inside your body. Whatever you do to the planet, you do to yourself. If you as a species stop polluting your earth, water and air, you will stop polluting your bodies. They are inextricably connected, as you can see. But this can all be reversed, as you can also see, and we will reverse all these conditions that are against life, when we come to the surface in the not too distant future. I am Mikos, Caretaker of the Earth.

Our Water Talks

Our shorelines are packed with the purest of sand, white colored and soft and crystal clear specs of the smoothest particles you have ever stepped on. Walking on our sandy beaches is akin to having the best foot massage possible. And we do walk on our beaches for this very purpose, for its massage soothes our feet and mind simultaneously. Our ocean's waves lap our shorelines with the purest and cleanest of water you have ever seen or tasted. And the temperature is always perfect for our bodies. Not too warm and not too cold. We walk into our oceans where it is shallow, and swim out great distances without ever getting tired or cold. No one here ever drowns. This is unheard of and unimaginable. We are all great swimmers, and our oceans and lakes support us so that we stay on top of the water.

Our water has consciousness, and talks to us while we are immersed in it. **Yes, our water talks.** When we swim, our water becomes part of our body, and we are one body, one ocean, swimming along the currents and through the waves. We merge ourselves completely with the water's consciousness, and our swim is a trip in consciousness itself. It is so much more than what you experience in your surface lakes and oceans, where the consciousness of your water has become so densified and polluted that it has lost its voice and vitality and life force. It weakly calls out to you, but you don't hear it. It calls out to you for help. It calls out to you to stop polluting it, to stop bombarding it with ELF sound waves, to stop the whaling ships and underwater experiments, and oil spills, and submarines, and cruise ships from destroying and poisoning its life force. But alas, it rests on deaf ears. For the children of Earth are still deaf to the destruction they are causing the Earth. It's only the greedy politicians who know what they are doing, and they do it purposely to destroy the Earth for their own personal gain, in the name of bolstering the economy. Everything is for the economy, and nothing for the Earth or its people. Families don't count anymore, only the state of the economy counts. You never hear about the 'state of the family' on the news, it's always the 'state of the economy' you hear about. Well, when there's no longer any families alive, there won't be an economy either.

So help yourself by helping your Earth. It's only through your returning your surface oceans and lands to their pristine state that you will return to a perfect economy where everyone lives in abundance and perfect health.

Our Inner Earth Oceans are Sanctuaries to all Marine Life

The Inner Earth's Oceans contain all of the life that's in the upper oceans, and more. Our oceans are teeming with life, and all of the marine forms live in harmony with one another.

All are on a vegetarian diet and do not hunt others. All live in harmony. All the marine life is very evolved compared to the life in the surface oceans. All are used to the peace and safety of our waters, and all are accessible to us. We all communicate directly to the Cetaceans and fish, and live cooperatively and in peace with one another.

Since we are all on a vegetarian diet, we don't hunt the Whales, go fishing or farm shrimp. Therefore, Mother Nature is free to evolve in our oceans and our oceans are sanctuaries to all ocean life. We just call to whomever we want to talk to, and they swim to our shores and converse with us. It would seem truly magical to you, but to us it is commonplace. **Remember, all of us in the Hollow Earth know we are ONE.**

There are numerous underwater caverns, where we go 'scuba' diving and explore the intricacies and complexities of life beneath the oceans. There are so many different kinds of organisms and plants and corals that are hidden in the ocean caverns that are beauteous to see. We love to dive and swim, explore and commune with the nature elementals in the oceans. There's a whole other civilization beneath our seas that we live in peace and cooperative partnership with. How wonderful to exist in a climate of peaceful exchange that we have forged beneath the Earth.

Your surface whales and dolphins sometimes swim through the underground ocean tunnels to visit and commune with us. They stay a short while and then return to the surface. They wish they could stay longer, but know their mission is above ground, and hesitatingly leave for the great swim upwards.

13. Food and Elements of Nature

Our Earth Gives All Life A Home To Evolve On

Greetings from the Hollow Earth! I am Mikos, speaking to you from my office in the Library of Porthologos, situated inside the Earth beneath the Aegean Sea. Today we will talk about our Earth, our dear planet that gives all life a home to evolve on. Know that your home is also the home of countless other species that depend upon it for shelter, food and a place to live. Your corporations act as if the land belongs to them alone, with no regard for other life forms. Space on Earth is designated for all species to share equally, for all are here to evolve their souls and all are here to enjoy their life spans. As this is especially true for humans, all other species have come to help and bolster the life of humans by giving them oxygen, food and clothing. All you have, is being given to you as gifts from other species. The trees give you oxygen, the animals give you clothing, and the crops give you food. All of these are live, conscious beings, here in service to Earth and to all life forms. Trees, animals, crops, plants, Cetaceans and all ocean life, all need their habitats kept intact in order for them to survive and evolve, just as humans need their homes to live in to carry on their lives.

It is a travesty to destroy the natural habitats of other living beings just to pave more roads, make more shopping centers, and erect more suburban tract homes. By cutting down trees and moving animals out of their homes, you destroy their lives, thereby endangering yours. For in order for all life to evolve, there must be an ecological balance on Earth. Humans have destroyed this delicate ecological balance, thinking only of themselves and not honoring the right of other life forms to claim their inheritance and their share of land and resources on Earth. This pushing off, and moving out, of other species is causing a severe imbalance to the Earth, which is leading to the devastation of flora and fauna, and ultimately to the destruction of all life everywhere.

For all life is interdependent and intricately interconnected. What happens to one happens to all; and mankind is now waking up and starting to realize this interconnectedness.

We, here in the Hollow Earth, have learned this many eons ago, and base our life on this connection to all life everywhere. This is also your connection to God. For once you realize your connection to all life, you automatically are reconnected to God, the Source of All That Is. And it is this connection that will evolve your soul and move you into your ascension. When all mankind awake to their connection to all other life, they suddenly find themselves connected to God and their trip home begins.

We have already made this trip, and find ourselves secure in the 'Garden of Eden' inside Earth. Paradise is the destination of your trip too, and many are now living lives of joy and abundance right here on the surface of Earth. You really don't have to go anywhere to enjoy your life fully. You just have to make your 'connection in' and everything you ever dreamed of will come to you effortlessly. For this is the way life was intended to be.

Here in the Hollow Earth, we watch and pray and send our Love to you daily. We encourage you to connect in consciousness with us, for through your connection we can send you our energy to energize your body and feed your spirit.

Food Takes on the Mass Consciousness of the Community It's Grown In

I am Mikos, calling to you from my Inner Sanctuary in the Inner Earth, where I dwell in peace and contentment for all God has given me. You, on the surface, live in misery, lack, and trepidation, because you have separated yourself from God, thinking that you know best, or more than the Creator. Your lives have been blessed with the riches and abundance of the Earth, and yet you turn away from Her, in your disdain, using your own methods of farming instead of Natures'. Mother Earth has always produced an abundance of crops for all who work with her, using Nature's Law of Rotation and Nature's Law of turning the soil into itself and letting it lie fallow to recover and restore its nutrients. By continual planting of the same crops over and over, dosed with toxic fertilizers and chemicals, you kill the rich nutrients of the Earth, leaving crops that are devoid of nutrition and devoid of the Life Force.

People of old always worked with the Devas, the Guardians of the soil; and by working together, and allowing the Earth herself to manage and make decisions for the growth of crops that are planted, the yields were always large — nay, enormous — and brimming with the force of life pulsing through each atom. It is this force of life in each atom and cell, this pulsation, this quickening, which is the Immortal Elixir of life. It is the secret of staying "young forever".

The Devas are returning to Earth after a long absence and are quietly helping those few people who are turning to them, to rebuild the soil with life enriching nutrients that will nourish and sustain the cells in our human bodies. The Devas are glorious beings who want to work with all humans, whether you farm or not, or just garden. They want to return to a partnership with you, so that all people can learn the magic of the soil, the magic of planting and harvesting again, the magic of growing your own food, in your own locality, for your own consumption. **Food shipped to you from other localities, from far away states, does not vibrate with your local surroundings or your own particular pulse of life.**

Everything is a reflection of your immediate surroundings, including your auras that surround you; and everything you touch or are near picks up your pulsating atoms, and these atoms become part of the soil and part of the vibration of everything you grow. So don't you think that you would be healthier to absorb only those vibrating atoms in your food that originate from your own self and from the community you vibrate with, rather than from an unknown locality that you are out of synchronicity with? There is so much to think of here, and much to understand about the nature of life, and how we all adapt to the particular locality we live in and how we become that locality. We are the environment that we live in, just as much as the crops we grow are.

It is confusing to your body cells to be ingesting foods from out of your immediate locale, because they do not resonate with your lifestyles, your thoughts, or your feelings. Instead, you imbibe, you actually "eat" other people's thoughts and feelings and they become yours — not knowing the danger and incompatibility this has on your digestive system and overall operation of all your organs, all your growth hormones, all your glands, and everything that makes you "you." Your ingesting of the thoughts of other people results in fears and phobias that aren't even your own, and then you wonder where this all came from.

Know that in order to have healthy and strong bodies, you need to feed them with only foods from your own local communities. This will enhance your life force and bring balance to your thoughts and feelings, because you will be reinforcing and strengthening your desires and dreams — which comprise the mass consciousness of a community.

This is why your world is out of sync, because it is out of sync with nature. Call on the Devas, ask them all to return, tell them you want to learn from them and work in tandem with them, to restore life to the soil and life to your bodies. Without this life force, your bodies decay and wither, and although your cells were meant to stay young and never age, they lack the life force to sustain themselves.

Your current civilization has moved further and further away from the soil, the trees, and the animals, into the ivy tower of technology, with no windows to look outside at their surroundings. They have closed the door to communing with nature, and wonder why they feel so alone and so needy, no matter how much money they have.

We implore you, Earth people, to return to Nature. She beckons you back to be one with her again, and to follow in the footsteps of your ancestors, the Native American Indians, who knew the land as part of themselves, who lived with nature, and honored and revered her bounty, and who learned from her, always using her own way to grow crops, and never forcing her to work against herself.

Spend time outdoors, not locked up in your houses. Spend time just sitting with the trees and walking in the woods, and notice the life force returning to you, invigorating you and balancing your emotional body. **Nature is a great antidote for your society's ills — and it's free for all to receive. You don't need to consult a physician for a prescription; the trees will dispense it to you for free. Why do you think they are here — only to grace your landscape?**

The trees are Majestic Beings, evolved beyond anything your thoughts can picture. And they wait for you to recognize them also as the stewards of the land, as the Cetaceans are the stewards of the sea, always giving you the oxygen you need, and absorbing the pollutants you create. And what do you do in return for this gift of life? You cut them down, you move them out of your way, and you ignore them. They are yearning to communicate with you, yearning to feel your touch and embrace you in their love and energy. Go to them, talk to them, sit with them, as they stand vigilant over your homes and communities as protectors of your very lives. Talk to them, and they will answer. They have been waiting eons to have humans reconnect to them again.

Nature will free you. You will regain your balance, you will regain your will to dream and to rebuild your lives in accordance with the Laws of Nature, not the laws of man.

We, here in the Hollow Earth, are one with nature, one with all life, and one with God. This is why we live such long lives and are so healthy. We know we are all a part of our planet, and our planet is a part of us. When we work with nature, we work as one. When we ignore nature, we ignore ourselves. This is a Universal Law that is crucial to your survival as a species.

We bring your attention to this, so you can protect your planet so that you have a home to evolve on. **Since you can't evolve in space, we wonder why you so blatantly destroy your home?**

You would marvel at the wonders in the Inner Earth, the wonders of beauty and the "down to earth" sensible lifestyles we have, all because we apply the Universal Law of the Oneness of all life. I bid you good day.

Our Fields of Grains

Our fields of grains sparkle and thrive and are perfectly touched by the "sun" and rain to produce the most luscious of crops that are so pleasing to our palates and so invigorating for our bodies. Our food pulses with the force of life, and when eaten by us, transfers the life force into our very cells, which results in perfect health and longevity of years.

This is the secret of life; this is the hidden fountain of youth you've all been looking for on your surface. It is found in the Earth herself, just waiting to give you its life force if you will but follow nature's laws of planting and harvesting crops, using only nature herself to direct the process and oversee the growth. With the great forces of nature working with you, you don't need to add anything to the soil, and the harvests are always magnificent in size and nutrients and taste.

This strength given us by our foods enables us to perform Herculean feats with our bodies that you would consider impossible. We can walk and run extremely long distances without tiring, and swim for hours at a time. We are not tired at the end of a day's "work", because nothing we do is "work". It is all joy and ease, and contentment is felt at the end of each day.

Our lives are truly wonderful, and we have much to feel blessed for. But we have created this utopia ourselves, and so can, and so will, you. For your future is to be glorious. **You are about to break through this density into heaven.** And this heaven is right here on Earth. Right now only half of the planet resides here, but soon the whole planet will be in the heaven you've been searching for. For **heaven is not in another place; its location is right here on Earth.** Right here where you live. You only have to bring it here through your higher consciousness. For heaven is just a frequency, and you are now rising rapidly toward accessing that frequency. And We, here in the Hollow Earth, are applauding your desire and determination to grow in awareness and reach the frequency of ascension that is plummeting to Earth from the Great Central Sun. Your Father/Mother, God and Goddess, Alpha and Omega, are bringing you home, back into their bosoms of love, where We will all dwell for the rest of eternity.

14. Our Environment and Weather

How Do You Control the Weather in the Hollow Earth?

Greetings on this fine winter day in 2003. We feel the climate changes from above, just as you do, even though we are physically removed from them and nestled snugly inside the Hollow Earth. For we track the weather conditions and anomalies on the surface, and can tell when a cataclysm (earth quake, hurricane, etc.) is about to occur. We are meteorologists too, and specialize in monitoring the weather conditions on the surface. This way, we can tell where pockets of darkness and negative thought forms that create weather imbalances are coming from. We then focus our love light on these areas to disperse and dematerialize them. This is one of the many contributions we render to the surface.

If surface folk knew the importance of keeping their mental and feeling bodies balanced, they could change the world overnight from one of chaos to one of peace. It's all in the balance. As each of you brings balance to your life, the Earth gains that measure and it goes out to all life, which in turn adds this amount of balance to their lives…and so it goes. It means to monitor and control your thoughts and feelings, just as you would monitor and control a science experiment in a lab to produce the desired results.

Well, think of your life as an experiment, and you being given the experience of learning to control all aspects of yourself. This is the key to a harmonious life and to peace on Earth. Each person plays such an integral role in bringing peace, that you would be amazed if you could 'actually see' how your thoughts and feelings go out into the world and touch others. It is a Law of Life that whatever you think and feel creates your reality and affects others as well – including all the other Kingdoms on Earth.

You are powerful, aren't you? Now harness your power into constructive building blocks that will bring peace to everyone around you and that will promote peace on Earth. It all starts with you, each individual on Earth. Take control of your life, and you can control the weather and receive the benefit of warm, sunshiny days, with gentle breezes that caress your skin. This is the 'true' weather control system, and we've installed it in the Hollow Earth. And you can install it for free on the surface, with 'no' installation fees.

Not only can you balance the weather using this technique, but you can balance your body and free it from stress and the imbalancing factors that cause disease. All these with no charge either. Everything you wish for, you can create from within yourself for free, and freely dispense it to others and to Mother Earth herself – thus healing all life everywhere. What a gift you have stored within you, and you can dispense your healing without ever spending thousands of dollars going to medical school; for you have already graduated. You're here on Earth to practice what you already know, and the knowledge is stored in the memory banks of your cells.

We always go within to our inner storehouse, to access all we need to live lives of peace and abundance. God's Light within us never fails. It is only your failure to go within to find the inner storehouse that keeps piling up for your use. By now, you have quite an oversupply just waiting for you to tap into and start bringing it into your outer lives.

Adama talks about the Oceans and Mountains in the Hollow Earth

The Earth's Interior is the mirror image of the surface foundation. Everything is in reverse order in the inside of the Earth. The mountain ranges are in direct proportion to the dimensions of the Earth's cavity, and tower above the landscape. The oceans are larger than life, and flow calmly and swiftly around the inside of the globe. The air is crisp and clean, and the sand is white. The Central Sun is dimmer than the sun on the outside, and reflects the Light from the Heavens.

The cities are all nestled in lush woodlands, overflowing with flowers and huge trees. There is green growth surrounding all man-made structures. Everything is in perpetual blossom and bloom. It is a land of wonder and beauty.

All is in perfect proportion to the size of the circumference of the interior. Everything is larger than life — even the great Beings who inhabit the interior are larger than the mortals on the outside. All is beauty, and all is in a heavenly state of bliss.

Just picture the interior foundation reflecting the exterior foundation; with mountain ranges higher, and the ocean currents swifter, and the green land growth lush beyond compare. You do not need to picture a change in the contour of the land. It is still in its pristine beauty, and replicates how life on the surface once was. The exact location of the mountain ranges and oceans is not necessary to know at this time. What is necessary to know is that this Inner World exists, and co-exists with the surface, under peaceful and contrary conditions.

Weather, Tunnels and Spaceports in the Hollow Earth

I am Adama speaking now. Know that cataclysmic weather conditions are in store for your surface population. Many negative thought forms are being released from your bodies and from the Earth, and these are causing drastic atmospheric unbalances, resulting in tornadoes, earthquakes, and other variable conditions.

Up north, where it's colder and the days are shorter, people will begin to see a change in their weather and seasonal patterns. The days will grow longer and the seasons will begin to merge into one another, just as they do in the Hollow Earth. In the Hollow Earth, there is a constant temperature in the low 70's. This "constant" temperature allows the people to live in relative ease and comfort, for no obstacles impede their activities.

The Hollow Earth is a Paradise, with tall, graceful mountains jutting into the "sky"; and large, clear, clean lakes and oceans that abound with life. The diet in the Hollow Earth is strictly vegetarian, and people are healthy, robust, and strong. They, too, have isolated themselves from the surface population, although they come and leave the Earth freely using the spacecraft that are kept there in the Spaceport in the inside of the Earth. So although they are inside the Earth, they have freedom and health, and abundance and peace — all the necessary components of life that you on the surface have been crying out for.

There is free travel between the subterranean cities and the Hollow Earth through the tunnels, using our electromagnetic trains that can take us from one part of the Earth to another in a fraction of the time it takes you on the surface. Our transportation is quick and efficient, and burns no fuels. Therefore, there's no pollution underground.

We long for the day when you on the surface can travel freely to the Hollow Earth, where you'll be greeted with great joy and love. It is this return, to the Land of Eden, that you are all crying out for. We, too, await this day, as all of us in the subterranean cities will join with you in the celebration, merging all our civilizations into One.

UNDERGROUND TUNNEL SYSTEM

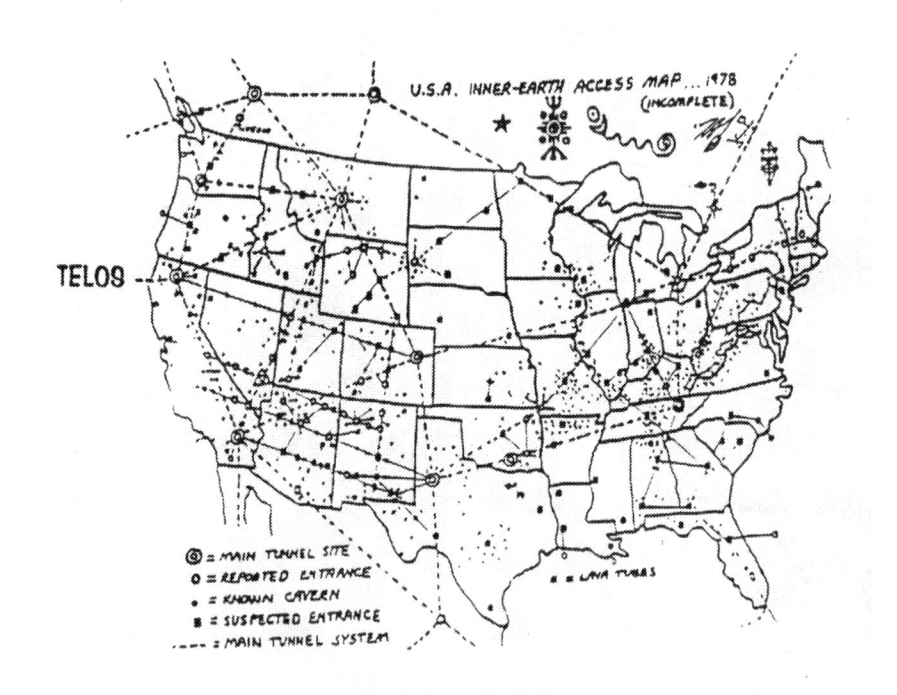

(Map drawn by Tal LeVesque)

There are tunnels intertwining throughout the planet, connecting every large city or state. The Inner Earth inhabitants can reach most of their destinations within hours, if not minutes. This underground network of passageways has been used for eons. They are more connected below than we are above. They can travel anywhere freely without making reservations, paying large sums of money or spending days at airports, train stations, or in cars.

15. Our Homes

All Our Buildings Are Round

Our library rooms are all environmentally harmonious with our outdoor surroundings, and all are open to the green of our outdoors and rich fragrances of our flowers. Our rooftops are open as well, as there are none. There is nothing above us to separate us from heaven. Our office room space is exposed to all the elements, and all the Hollow Earth elements harmoniously and joyously intermingle and interact in a state of divine perfection. So we don't need rooftops to protect ourselves from them, as they work directly with us – not against us. And because all our buildings are round, we never have to dust, because dust never accumulates. We live dust free lives in our circular buildings and homes. Geometric shapes have certain properties, and in a circle the energy freely moves and revolves, carrying dust particles along with it so that the dust never settles in corners – since a corner does not exist in a circle. So as a dust particle moves into a room, the energy flow also carries it out. It is more efficient than a vacuum cleaner, because a storage bag isn't necessary. Soon this architectural principle will be prevalent on Earth, and all your structures will be circular in shape.

Jewels, Diamonds, and Crystals

We reside here, in the Hollow Earth, amongst great richness, and live in great palaces infused with Light. To you, it would seem as a fantasyland, but to us it is real, as we created it from our own God Selves. We created homes for Gods and Goddesses, and this is where we dwell.

We dwell amongst richness your eyes cannot yet conceive of. Every possible convenience is at our fingertips and our environment is more beautiful than you can imagine. Our homes are set in the lushness of the countryside that abounds all around us, and are built right into the natural environment, surrounded by lakes and streams.

We have no cities like yours. We have only "country" that never ceases to amaze even Us. The trees and flowers are vibrant with pulsating hues and shapes, and caress our homes and land. Everything is "monumental", as you would term it. Even our trees and mountains are double the height of yours, and of course our bodies are taller and larger in frame. The width and girth of our figures more than doubles yours, and our fruits and vegetables are huge in comparison to yours. All our foods are organic, as we are in tune with Mother Earth, and she personally directs their growth.

We live in grand palaces made of crystallized stones that are embedded with jewels from the Earth. These crystallized stones create a magnetic field and radiance that nurtures and balances our bodies, and fills us with the Life Force emanating from the Great Central Sun of our Universe. All things in our homes radiate the purity of God, and tune us to God's vibrations. For it is God's love that fills our homes and God's love that creates the richness in our lives.

Our homes are round and translucent, and blend into the countryside. By outward appearances they give us total privacy. But once within, we can see out in all directions around us. This gives us a spacious feeling of vision, rather than being "locked in", as you are on the surface. Not only can we see out of our homes, but we can see out beyond the Earth, to the Stars in the sky. Our vision has no boundaries or barriers, wherever we are in the Hollow Earth. Our eyes and senses are free to roam the Universe, while our bodies remain inside the globe.

We Live Inside Caverns

Now that you are familiar with the Hollow Earth, we can "dig" further into your credibility and introduce another factor of our living arrangements underground.

Underground, we do not live out in the open spaces the way you do on the surface. Our Hollow Earth cavity is pristine because we don't tread upon her inner surface nor build upon her. We don't have shopping malls and expanses of highways nor towering buildings. We live inside caverns, with openings facing inward toward the open, wide spaces of the Hollow cavity inside the Earth. Sure, we travel inside the cavity on our electromagnetic vehicles that levitate a few inches above the ground – but never touch the ground. We walk softly on the earthen paths and run along the streams, rivers and oceans, and climb the towering mountains. But that is the extent of our foot contact with the terrain. The rest we leave to nature's devas and elementals, as it is their land, too.

All our living activity takes place within our inner caverns, which are vast and wide and high and composed of crystalline rocks and gemstones and crystal arches radiating full-spectrum colored rainbows of sparkling light into our cavern atmosphere. Our walls are lined with natural rainbow-hued waterfalls, humidifying the air with the vibrancy and song of its water cascading down. Yes, our water sings – and its chorus brings our body cells into harmony, so that our bodies are always vibrating to our water and crystalline surroundings that keep us energized and vibrant all day long. We need little sleep, because our cells are always tuned and in harmony to the natural rhythm of Mother Earth herself. When you are tuned like a tuning fork, then you carry the full life force of our Mother, and your battery never runs down. Hence, there is little need for the long hours of sleep such as you experience it. You are drained and run-down after a day in your "sweatshops," but we are always as vibrant at the end of our days as we are when we begin them. We live "in" and "with" the Earth, whereas you live "outside" and "separate" from her. Hence, you are "cut off," while we are a "part" of her. This is the big difference.

Humanity was not meant to live on the Earth's rooftop, but inside her interior terrain. This was a big experiment that, unfortunately, backfired and resulted in alienation and "deep" separation from her life-giving body. Soon this will all be changed and remedied, and people will be living inside her, not on top of her. **You live inside your house, not on its rooftop, don't you? Well, the same analogy applies to the Earth.** There are vast caverns throughout the interior of the Earth, many already inhabited by many different kinds of beings who have been living unobtrusively in them for millennia.

Your Spiritual Hierarchy has been preparing housing for you inside these vast, uninhabited caverns in Earth's interior, and when it's time, you will all be moved en masse into them to continue your present incarnation inside Earth, not "on" her. You will encounter a "whole" new way of living that is wholesome and rich and perfect in every way. It will expand your consciousness and expand your horizon, and your horizon will be an inner horizon vaster than when you walk outdoors on the surface. A whole new horizon is waiting for you to experience.

Events will start happening fast now, as time is speeding up even faster as world karma is playing itself out. Just ride with the tide and know you are safe wherever you are. You are all being directed and guided from within, and you are all being provided for. What you witness through your media is only a "play," a drama that they want you to believe is real, just because the actors are real. But the actors are just "playing out their part" in the world's drama, and this is the biggest "hit" yet of the new millennium, playing on your TV and movie theater screens everywhere. Just turn the knob off, go within yourself, and feel and focus on world peace. Peace is the real movie, and the only "reel" to watch.

Soon, you will see us, and soon you, too, will be living perfectly suited to your new way of life.

Inner Earth Caverns Will Be Humanity's New Home

Greetings from Earth's caverns! I am speaking to you today from my cavern inside the interior crust of the Hollow Earth.

Yes, there are caverns inside the Hollow Earth just as there are under the surface. The Earth is filled with caverns; everywhere you go on the planet there are caverns of such multitude and magnitude that the entire surface population can be comfortably housed inside.

In fact, this is how it is on all other planets in your solar system and beyond. The occupants all reside in inner domiciles, protected from the winds and sun of their solar system. This, indeed, will be the next step for humanity - to take residence inside the Earth herself for protection from the elements and forces of Nature that are bearing down on you from the outer atmospheric shell of Earth, and wreaking havoc on your cities in the form of hurricanes, tornados, earthquakes, winds, severe heat and cold extremes in temperature. The Earth is in the process of ridding herself of all pollution and may go through drastic measures to do so.

This cleansing of her surface will also give those the opportunity to leave the Earth plane early and to continue their learning in the newly established temples and universities on the Inner plane.

The hardships will enable those who stay to more quickly wake up to Earth's call and work with her and not against her. It will be a great opportunity for soul growth on Earth, and rare lessons will be available.

The caverns inside the Earth have been readied to accommodate the Earth's surface population, and they will all be brought inside when the time comes.

There's a web of tunnels crisscrossing throughout (or rather "through-in") the Earth's interior that will connect all caverns by electromagnetic vehicles that levitate and do not ever touch the ground as they whisk you through them from location to location. All is lit up in a soft iridescent glow, illuminating everything clearly while radiating a feeling of warmth inside the tunnel passageways.

The caverns will mirror your surface, except, of course, for the oceans, which you will have to travel into the Hollow Earth to access. The Hollow Earth is not that far away from the inner caverns – just minutes by electromagnetic vehicles, and they're all free. There's no transportation costs inside the Earth. In fact, there's no money at all. All is on a barter system and transportation is always free to all. You will be able to travel at will and finally explore the depths of the Earth as you begin to experience the depths of your own Being simultaneously. You, who choose to stay, are in for a great adventure in love and light and will witness the expansion of your universe from here on Earth.

16. DNA and Inner Doors of Consciousness

All People on Earth are from the Same DNA Blueprint

My dear friends on the northeastern surface of America, I am Mikos, your friend from beneath the Aegean Sea, here to speak to you today about LOVE; love for your people and love for your planet.

All people on Earth are from the same DNA blueprint, but evolution has created different outward appearances. So your appearance is determined dependent upon your location. These are not differences, just variations of body appearance. For within the body, lies the soul; and the souls of all humans come from the Divine Creator of All – are indeed a part of the Divine Creator - just embellished with Earthly characteristics and Earthly experiences that become different and distinct over eons of time. So what you see in others, is their Earthly sojourn, so to speak, and not their heavenly garment. This has confused humans for millennia, and resulted in separation and wars, instead of unity and peace.

We admonish you to look through God's eyes when you look at others, and see only God standing in the midst of you. You will see how rapidly your world conditions would change, if all would only look through God's eyes, always, which really are the eyes you look through when cleared of Earthly density and fear.

Take long walks through the countryside and breathe in the fragrant green-filled air. For the green of the countryside pulsates with the healing atoms that you all need so desperately to recover from the chaos of the city and your workplaces. For your city life depletes your life force, which the Trees and Nature can restore. The Trees are eager to help you, eager to give you their life-breathing oxygen that your city life consumes as rapidly as the Trees produce it. So rapidly, that now there is a great oxygen deficit on your surface and you all are feeling the effects of being oxygen-starved, due to your commerce and way of life.

We in the Hollow Earth are out in Nature 24 hours a day, as this is our <u>only</u> way of life. This is how we live because our surroundings are totally nature-made. We have no pollution producing cities. We have no asphalt or concrete suffocating Mother Earth's body. We have only trees and shrubs and grass and flowers everywhere we look. We have an abundance of pure oxygen, which renews and rebuilds our bodies 24 hours a day, resulting in our great strength and great energy levels, and clear thinking.

We wait for the time when you will be allowed to come 'down' and visit us, and witness for yourself our divine living conditions – which you can also create on the surface. Don't despair, for all in heaven are here to help you bring this heavenly way of existence down to Earth, so that all surface dwellers will at last experience the beauty and joy that was originally intended at the outset of this grand experiment on Earth, over 14 million years ago. I am Mikos, and bid you good day.

Feel Your Heart As It Beats

'Feel your heart as it beats
Listen to your pulse as it throbs to the rhythm of life
Feel your blood as it courses through your body
Carrying oxygen and nutrients to every cell

You are a self-contained storehouse of life
You are a microcosm of the Universe
You are a replica of God
All of life pulses through you
All knowledge is contained within you
All can be accessed by you

Just go within and ask, and then listen, and then feel,
and then you will know
For all answers are within you
For you are within ALL
And ALL IS ONE'

The Living Library of All Knowledge is Located WITHIN Each of You

I greet you today in the name of the One Creator of All That Is, the Living God within us all. Know that your distance from us is not far, just a few kilometers in space, and although this distance physically divides us, we are as close as the leaves are to the tree, we are as close as the wind that brushes your face, for our consciousness flows out from the depths of the Earth and reaches you to caress and bless you every moment.

We came here specifically to help this great Earth evolve and to have a home for our own evolution at the same time; and to bring you, who live on the surface, up into the higher realms of light where we can all meet and be together as One. For with our merging of consciousness we become a great force of Light that can bring all of us into higher and higher realms where all the avatars await us. So move up with us in consciousness, and flow with us through the Earth and read our thoughts on the return flow, so we can converse with one another as was meant to be; our conversing and our meeting is what will move all of us into higher dimensions of light.

We come before you this day in all our glory and splendor, bringing forth all our wisdom and cheer, to cheer you on your path, the ever winding path that never ends, that leads only upward and onward into the glory of God, the glory of God within you. **For within you is ALL. All the answers you are seeking, all the explanations you need.** It is all there, within your vast human temple that stores all the information of the cosmos, and we beckon you to access it.

We beckon you to follow us in thought, and as you do, we can help you resolve and solve all your earthly cares, all your earthly problems. For now that you know we're here, just call on us; we will hear you and we will respond. For this is our mission, this is our dream, to connect with each one of you on the surface, and gently lead you and guide you into the light of your higher self, the light where you actually dwell, the place where all is stored and all awaits your opening to the doors of information that lie hidden within your very being.

All life on Earth at this time has access to their inner doors of consciousness that need only be nudged to turn the lock and open. So, move these doors and open them, and you will find us here, ready to walk with you into Eternity. We are ever beaming our lights to you, we are ever beaming our love to you, and we are ever beaming our thoughts to you. Catch them, and return them to us.

We are nestled snugly in our hearths, in our homes, inside the Earth, where we are very safe and very secure, and we offer this security and this snugness to you. We offer this to you in hopes that you will follow us, and we will take you into the heart of God, which resides in your very own heart space, your very own temple of Light.

We love you all very deeply. We know of your dreams and we know of your desires to live peaceful, abundant lives. So please travel with us, as we explore fully all that there is and all that you can achieve. Just know that this exploration comes from within you; you don't need to go anywhere. **You can explore the depths of your very own soul and the universe from right where you're sitting.** There's no need for physical travel of any kind. Just beckon to us and we will take you there. Because once you merge your consciousness with ours, we are One. And you can travel with us. We can travel together to the outermost reaches of space and to the innermost reaches of your soul. And we can unite in one consciousness and blast our way to the Stars.

The Living Library of all knowledge is located within you. From this access point within you, you have your fingertips reaching all the knowledge there is.

> **You don't have to physically
> turn the pages of a physical book;
> just turn the pages within your soul
> to rediscover all the wisdom
> and all the knowledge
> that ever was and
> ever will be.**

You do this by going into meditation and consciously connecting with the God Source that you are, and calling on your friends in the Subterranean Cities and the Hollow

Earth, your Family of Light, to be here with you and to explore the Hidden Realms with you, until the hidden realms become exposed and open pages for you to read. These are the same hidden realms that you explore nightly in your etheric body, as you leave the Earth plane and are once again free, free to be all you are meant to be. So be with us in your thoughts and explore the Hollow Earth in your visions, and see us just waiting for you to connect with us so we can take you on the journey of your life into the Hollow Globe and out to the Stars.

17. Synchronicity, Imagination, and Rebirth

Synchronicity Is the Result of Unity Consciousness

I am Mikos, and today I will talk about our lives within the Globe, and how synchronicity guides our every movement and thought, for we are within the Unity Consciousness that prevails in our Universe. And once within this frequency of consciousness, you have access to all thoughts and information that exist within this wave band. This is the path that is opening to all surface dwellers. It is this path that, if you follow it, will lead you into emergence with all of us underground, and all life in the Universe.

Once you are within Unity Consciousness, all falls into place, as you are in synchronicity with all life everywhere in the Universe – not just on Earth. This is how opportunity comes to you, 'out of the blue'. Well, the 'blue' is the Universe, and once your path becomes known to 'All', 'All' is at your beck and call to arrange the instances and occurrences and resources you need to complete your mission on Earth.

It is being in the Universal flow of our Universe. This is where We exist, as We live Underground. We are in contact with all life in our Universe, and can see and hear and feel all that occurs. This is why our lives are so magical Underground; it's not the depth of the Earth that determines this, but the width of our consciousness – and our consciousness expands with our Universe. The Universe and We are ONE.

And so are you ONE with All That Is. And as the incoming energies flow and integrate within you, your connection with life will increase, until you become fully connected –

resulting in Unity Consciousness. Once this occurs, **MAGIC BECOMES COMMONPLACE,** as your life absorbs the magic of being connected again to all life, everywhere. And you suddenly find yourself in God's arms – fully secure and fully protected.

This is where the intense energies, being directed to you from the Great Central Sun of our Galaxy, are taking you. They are taking you back home to the frequency you all left behind when you came to Earth. We, in the Hollow Earth, carried this frequency with Us, and because of our seclusion we were able to maintain our Unity Consciousness, and have been waiting for you to join us. Once you make this connection, all Earth goes up in flame – the Ascension Flame – and moves up into a higher dimension of evolution as quick as a wink. No time elapses between being 'there' (on the surface) and being 'here' in Unity Consciousness. So make this trip with us, for the journey will take your soul to Nirvana.

In the Hollow Earth, all we think, we create; for we are conscious of each thought and conscious of its outcome. Therefore, we can create exactly what we desire to enhance our already perfect lives. It's not 'hit' or 'miss' like it is on the surface, where you create both what you want and what you don't want, thereby bringing confusion and difficulties into your lives at the same time you're trying to perfect it - and it then seems that you are 'going nowhere'. We understand this process you go through, as we've been watching you for millennia, on our underground computer screens. You take one step forward and one step back, as you try to resolve all the difficulties and break through all the obstacles in your life.

Soon all the destructive forces will be revealed and removed from the surface, so that you are not picking up and reflecting their negativity into your lives. The veil of Maya has been pierced, and you will begin seeing the politicians and laws for what they really are — which are barriers to life, not promoters as they profess to be. We have no negative interferences in the Hollow Earth, this is why our lives mirror perfection. And soon the surface will have no negative interference, for God's energy will not integrate with negativity, and these negative entities will not survive the influx of energies which will only increase in intensity. The Earth's ascension is now assured, and your desire to live only in the Light is fully assured too. Once you cross this 'energy line', you will suddenly discover Us and all life everywhere in our Universe. It has only been the veil of maya that has caused this separation in your perception of what exists and what doesn't exist. It is your field of vision that has been blurred – for we have always been here in your time – waiting for you to put in the corrective lenses of higher consciousness that will allow you to 'see' us.

We know you as our brothers and sisters who have temporarily lost your way over the last 12 million years of surface time. Through your consciousness, you are finding your way back to who you really are, and defining the kind of life you would really want to live. The life you live now seems like freedom to your blurred vision, but as your higher consciousness focuses the 'lens of life', you are seeing that this freedom is really slavery in disguise. When you have to work long hours for basic necessities that are really free, then you are in slavery – you are chattel. The electromagnetic grids surrounding Earth can supply you with all the energy you need for free. Your governments know this, and they use it for themselves. It is their way to keep you in debt. Indebtedness is slavery, not freedom.

The longer the hours you spend daily on your jobs, the more unbalanced your lives become. It isn't the money you need, it's the time to reflect on your lives and time to spend outdoors in Nature. This is the meaning of Freedom — having the time to bring your lives to fruition, to bring your dreams into your reality, to bring your lives back into balance and to bring your families back together again into a strong framework of unity.

In the Hollow Earth, our families are in total harmony and we support one another fully in everything we do. We always have our evening meals together, and always have time to sing and dance after dinner. We really understand the term 'fun', and it is a large part of our lives.

We dictate these messages to you, to give you 'life support' from the Hollow Earth. We are your 'life support system' from Underground, and we will continue our flow of energy to you, until you have fully 'recovered' from your surface life and make the transition in consciousness to our higher realm of existence.

Your Internal Light

We are combining our light into one mighty beacon and sending it through the crust to your surface population where it is received in their hearts.

Our life inside the Earth is always warm, sunny, and peaceful, and our spirits are always dancing with the Light of God inside. This internal reflection of the Light of God is what illuminates our minds and bodies and forms a halo of glowing light around us emanating from within.

You, too, can externally reflect your internal light. Just concentrate on your electronic current of Light energy running through your spine and magnify it through you. Know that this current connects you to the Great Central Sun, instantly electrifying you with the great Light of a thousand suns. Just see it, feel it, and know it. You are a mighty SUN. Your light alone can power all the appliances and electrical generators on Earth. This is how powerful you all are. And once you all come into your "knowing" and "discovery" of yourself, you won't need to pay electric and heating bills, for you will provide your own internal heat and your own light, so that the elements around you adapt to your vibrational flow and raise up all life within your energy field. This is true mastership, this is the "true" you.

So focus only on the Light and Love within you, and slowly and gradually you will raise the frequency of our sweet Earth into a rising ascension tide which cannot be stopped, but will only gain momentum and velocity, and like a mighty ocean wave will crash on the beaches of the 5th dimension, spilling you all onto its shores.

I am Mikos, part of the ocean tide that is showering you with our wave of Love from below.

Imagination Is The Real Substance Of The Universe

Greetings from Earth's interior! I am Mikos of the silver Light, speaking to you from the Library of Porthologos, deep inside the Earth. The Light is so bright inside our home, that it shines and sparkles like silver rays of light. All our lives we've lived among riches and splendor, and wonder how it could have eluded you on the surface? If you just look around, you will see the abundance and beauty of the Earth, and yet you've failed to mirror it in your lives. Instead you mirror the opposite of Earth's beauty. You mirror the lack and bleakness that you've created within yourselves, and think this to be the true picture of life. As your spiritual sight develops, you will begin to see the true identity of all the life that surrounds you; and then with a shocking awakening you will start out-picturing your 'real' surroundings and bring heaven to Earth. It is that simple. For heaven has always existed around you and within you, waiting for you to 'see' it.

You've created your own prison bars around your life stream, and now it is time to dissolve them with your higher vision. See right through them, and as you do, they will be obliterated by your higher sight frequency, never to return. This is how you see out into the Universe – by looking through all your past pre-conceived thoughts and beliefs and focusing on the beauty of the <u>whole</u> Universe; which you know is there if you can only penetrate it with your sight. You do this through your imagination, which isn't imagination at all, but 'imaging' or focusing on what really exists around you. You've been taught that imagination is unreal – but on the contrary, imagination is very real. It is the real substance of the Universe and is how you can see all of existence while your feet still stand on Earth.

It is like 'x-ray' vision, and it is real. It is the way to see beyond ordinary sight. If you're attuned to God, you will see the beauty and truth of all existence as you concentrate your mind on it, and let it come into your imagination. For come it will, with all the beauty and splendor that you can 'imagine'. It is only your thoughts that can deplete it of its magnitude, or close it off. It is only your ancient belief system that shuts you out from the rest of existence that is teeming around you.

So open your eyes from within your imagination, and let them roam the planets and galaxy, and you will know for a certainty that 'you are not alone', anywhere you go. For life, in all its myriad forms and dimensions, is surrounding you everywhere – all attuned to different frequencies of consciousness. But you can feel the space around you, as it is charged with prana, the nutritional and energetic spark of life. Prana can free you from your dependence on food, and can fill you with its life force. All advanced civilizations on other star systems live on prana, as St. Germain does when he visits Earth in his physical body.

Prana is the substance of the Universe, and will keep your body youthful and perfectly nourished forever. As you further awaken to who you are, imagine prana flowing into your crown chakra from a tube opening and going straight through your body down into the Earth. Concentrate and 'imagine' the prana coming into you, for it will return your body to physical perfection if you can start the flow of it again and maintain it.

We, in the Hollow Earth, are nourished by prana, although we delight in eating our 'homegrown' foods too. We are healthy and strong, and never sick a day in our lives. Headaches and stress are unknown to us, for all we feel is the peace and serenity we out-picture from our surroundings.

As you rise in consciousness, you will feel more and more of the beauty and perfection of life around you, and will be able to express it through your form and feelings and thoughts until it becomes as real to you as your old self is to you now. I am Mikos, always blazing my diamond light to you.

Spring of Rebirth

I am waiting for you in the Library of Porthologos, in the center of the Hollow Earth. We welcome you today, and are joyous to make our Sunday connection to you through the telepathic hotline. This hotline gives you access to our thoughts and our feelings, even though we are way below ground. And in the return loop, we access yours. It's a circuitous loop that connects us fully and completely as we merge our thoughts together as one.

Today it is Sunday, and as we gaze up to the stars, we feel heaven below. For heaven is where your heart is, although your body resides on Earth. April is a wonderful month of rebirth. It is the Spring of our souls, budding forth with new life and new fragrances and new hope for a new future. All life is decked out in buds and blossoms and garments of green, ready to burst forth into magnificent flowers and bushes and trees with the most fragrant of aromas. It is the turning point of the seasons, and all life waits in anticipation for this glorious event, just as all humanity waits for their consciousness to bud and bloom and open to the scent and sight and sounds of the heaven world that surrounds you. You are all prepared for a great re-birth of life, a regeneration and rejuvenation of your bodies and souls that will catapult you into the higher dimensions of life, where you will find us waiting for you. And we have waited so long. The Spring of life is finally here, and all Earth is now blossoming into the diamond petals of the creator.

Your entry into Light has been slow and tedious, but time has speeded up, and now you are where the flow of heaven can reach into your souls and permeate your cells with the diamond light of the Creator.

A New Golden Age
My dearest residents on Earth, I am speaking to you from the Inner Chambers of the Library of Porthologos located beneath the Aegean Sea deep inside the opening in the Center of the Earth.

The Light on the surface is expanding at hyper-speed and exponentially increasing faster than we can believe. You are all in for the "ride" of your lives, racing to catch up in consciousness with your unseen brothers and sisters living inside the Earth. We can hardly wait for your masses to reach our level of consciousness, for this is when our whole Earth explodes into a Star of Great Light, and with one leap you finally reach the 5th dimension where you can see into the Hollow Earth and see us with your new eyesight. You will be so surprised at all that you see around you and up in the heavens that you never saw before.

We are so grateful to all surface dwellers for their receptivity to the Light, and for allowing the Spiritual Hierarchy to keep increasing the increments of Light to the planet. It is only with your receptivity that the Light can so intensely fill your Earth and reach your bodies. Your eons of living lives of limited consciousness are over, and your bodies are gearing for return to full consciousness. You are at the threshold of a new Golden Age, one that is filled with only light and perfection and abundance and one that is destined to last forever.

You are the New Guardians of the Earth as the Cetaceans have passed the torch on to you – and you can finally take it and run with it in complete abandonment and joy. We are your neighbors down in the Earth, but our hearts are as close to you as if we were living next door. Soon our doors will be open to you, and you can come "down" for a visit. We, in turn, will be ringing your doorbell and coming for tea. What a glorious merging of civilizations this will be. There is only hope for a future of Love and Peace - for nothing else can exist. The prophets have prophesized this time for Earth, and now it is here.

The darkness is receding and the power moguls and cabals are retreating. They have been given the order to retreat from their posts of power and control or face the consequences. They will be removed. There will be many changes in store for all the governments on Earth, as the time for the implementation of the Divine Plan for Peace is at hand.

Return of the Christ Consciousness

Greetings. It is Mikos, your brother from the Hollow Earth, bringing you glad tidings for the ascension wave about to sweep the surface and funnel you into the Fifth Dimension of Light and Love and everlasting Peace. We bless you from below, as we feel the flow of energy engulfing our planet and all life in and on it.

Every living specie will be catapulted into a new world of Love and Light — a world where all can continue their everlasting evolution into Eternity, free from constraint and limitations and poverty and wars.

It is "now," dear ones, the Kingdom of God is at hand, just as Jesus predicted. The return he spoke about is the return of the Christ Consciousness within your heart flame and not somewhere up in a cloud.

So stand erect, feel your sovereignty, and connect with your Holy Christ Self, bringing it fully into your physical body and experiencing the strength and understanding that surpasses all. Feel us within you, for indeed we are a big part of you, as you are a part of us.

Your God-Selves are ready to take dominion within your hearts and minds, and this will bring your consciousness fully in union with us – where you will be able to perceive our world, even as you remain in yours.

We are feeling your closeness and waiting for your consciousness to ignite with ours into one blazing light, bringing all surface humanity into the "Father's house" where there are "many mansions" that Jesus spoke of.

As you make this trip "up" in consciousness, you will also be going "down" simultaneously, enabling you to see us as clearly as you see the house across the street. You will be able to see everything that exists in your solar system and galaxy. You are so close and we are so overjoyed at your progress and your ability to absorb so much Light so quickly. We cheer you on from below and wait for the pleasure of your company. We are ready to receive you into our homes and physically embrace you in our arms. We wait and pray for your entry into our realm of Light. I am Mikos, speaking to you on behalf of the citizens of Catharia.

18. Earth and Crystals

Our Earth Herself Is A Crystal

I am Mikos, and we are gathered around you in synchronicity, beaming our love and protection to you as you sit at your table taking this transmission. Know that our minds are melded and our hearts are One.

Today we will talk about the Crystals inside the Earth, including the one you hold in your hand. There is so much more to Crystals than what your eye perceives, for Crystals are Living Beings too. They are pure consciousness that holds memories of All That Is. They literally hold the events of the world.

Crystal energy is what vibrates the Earth, your body, and your cells. It is the vibrating force of the Universe that brings all life together as One pulse. Our pulses, and the pulses of all life forms, beat to this vibration, for it is this vibration that beats the hearts of life forms, animate and inanimate. For although we term crystals and rocks and stones as inanimate, they have a vibration that is in synchronicity with the Earth. And when we hold a crystal in our hand, it fine tunes our connection and pulse to the Earth — the Mother of all life here.

Our thoughts are pulsations of energy that emanate from us in waveforms that are either in tune with our surroundings or out of tune, depending upon our vibration. Since most of Earth, at this time, is still "out of beat", so to speak, with the forces of Nature, you can bring yourself back into the rhythm of Nature by surrounding yourselves and your homes with crystals.

Holding a crystal while you meditate is the best way to guarantee that your energy will be in harmony with the

Earth. And when your energy is in harmony with the Earth, you become aligned with the Earth's magnetic grid lines, and can access "All That Is" — for "All That Is", is in perpetual flow to Earth and to yourselves, if you are tuned to her frequency. We think this will help you understand the importance of having crystals in your homes, and carrying them when you go outside, either around your necks or in your pockets or purses. For they emit a protective field of resonating light around you, that cannot be penetrated by anything less than this light frequency.

Crystals are much like the trees, in the respect that they, too, are waiting for you to acknowledge them as "Living Beings" encased in stone, who are ready and eager to communicate with you and become a part of your life. They have so much to offer you, as they "step up" your vibration to levels where you are no longer feeling only the third dimensional density, but consciousness levels where you bypass third dimension and rise to higher levels of awareness, where all life waits for your entrance so that you can finally "see and feel" beyond your physical five senses and experience the multidimensionality of who you, as humans, truly are.

This is how We operate inside the Earth. We are always resonating with our crystals and matching their frequency, which is why we are able to exhibit our multidimensionality inside the Earth — because this is the only frequency we know. We always are in its crystalline flow, and we always are pulsing with our crystalline surroundings and Mother Earth's crystalline pulse rate. You, too, on the surface can match our "beat" by tuning in to us, here in the Earth's crystalline core, and keeping crystals in your homes and pockets.

All life, everywhere, is one great flow of Crystalline Light Energy. Planets who are in this synchronized flow are of the

Light, and planets who are not in this flow remain discordant and out of balance with the rest of the Universe. Earth is gradually raising her vibratory rate, and as the energy coming to you from our Great Central Sun speeds up, so does your vibratory rate, until you once again pulse with the synchronicity of our Universe. This will be one mighty pulse beat, which will move our ENTIRE Universe into a greater state of ultra-multidimensional consciousness, far surpassing its present state of consciousness, and beyond anything that anyone residing in this Universe has ever known before.

So meld yourselves with us in consciousness, as you allow your cells to resonate with ours through your imagining of us and your visions of us and your thoughts of us. These are REAL connections, although on your surface your imaginations are still considered unreal. **In reality, it is your imagination that propels you into higher states of awareness, where other life forms dwell.** You can actually "see" the fairies and gnomes and elves and devas through your imagination of them, for your imagination is another one of the senses that you will soon reclaim and begin experiencing more frequently again, until you imagine or remember all that you forgot.

So beat with us in frequency, feel our hearts merged with your heart, until we are only One heart. This is how you will traverse great expanses of space, and can be with us in consciousness. It is the fastest kind of travel in existence anywhere.

Everything in the Hollow Earth Is Constructed of Crystals

I am here to talk about our connection to the Universe, and your connection to all life everywhere. We are seated in our room in the Porthologos Library, looking out at the Stars, the Stars of heaven as they float silently by us. For even as we sit under the ground we can see out into the Universe in all directions at once. Our hearts and minds are attuned to the Creator, the Source of all Oneness and connector to all life.

We love our Earth, and as we live inside her, we are privy to all information that ever was — and to all events currently taking place on the surface as well as on other solar systems in our Galaxy. We capture, or record, these events in our Crystal Projectors, and file them away for safe keeping in our extensive library.

All our records are ancient, by your standards, as your lifetimes are so short compared to ours. But these "ancient" events existed in our lifetime, since we are eons of years old in the same body, and therefore occurred during our lifetime. This gives us a different perspective of life — one that honors and reveres the Earth and all life everywhere. Because we have lived through so many ages that have taken place on the surface, we have seen and experienced the connectiveness of all life everywhere.

Which brings us back to Crystals. The evolution of Crystals is ancient also, as they have always existed and are the witness to all events on Earth. They, themselves, have recorded all the events on Earth and stored them within their crystalline network of "nerves" that can hold voluminous amounts of information.

These crystals are very evolved Beings, whose mission it is to record all that transpires on Earth, so that all that has transpired can be played back on our Crystal Projectors and learned from. For all life is a learning experience, and without the knowledge and wisdom of the past, how do you expect to learn and advance your evolution? **Your books are all filled with misinformation, compiled by mankind's opinions and beliefs and theories that have little resemblance to actual conditions or facts.** So all you learn doesn't give you a clue as to the real nature of Earth, the Universe, or "you".

Whenever we want to learn something and apply it to our lives, we go into the Crystal Recording Room and play back the sequence of events that will lead us to the information and wisdom we need to resolve any problem or increase our understanding of events and our lives. This is important for you, our Earth brothers and sisters; for you, too, need to have this information available to you so that you can see how your elected government officials have mismanaged the Earth's resources, and have kept you in virtual survival struggle mode for eons. Your lives are so controlled and your freedoms so diminished that you don't even know it, because it's all that you've known, and you label it democracy, equated with freedom.

How the wool has been pulled over your eyes to keep out the Light of the Universe, and imprison you on this small island floating in space! For although you can't see out, or hear the Earth calling to you, or feel the love of the trees as you scurry by them in your frantic pace of life, know that all life, everywhere, is aware of your plight and has come to your rescue to wake you up out of your deep Slumber of the Ages so that you can regain your conscious remembrance of who you are, why you are here on Earth, and the important part you play in bringing Earth out of her density and into a higher realm of Light where you will experience real "freedom", firsthand.

Your crystals can help you make this jump in consciousness, in a miniscule amount of time. Just hold them close to you, and they imprint their wisdom into your heart in "no time" at all, and raise your vibration to a place where you can readily access all the knowledge and wisdom that has been gathered throughout all time. Your crystals, no matter what size they are, can move you all into a higher state of awareness.

We, in the Hollow Earth, are surrounded by our crystals in every "walk of life" and every place we go. Our homes, transportation, work places, cultural complexes, everything is constructed of crystals and surrounded by crystals. Our buildings literally glow with Crystal Light, and our body's glow increases as we advance in our evolution. For love and wisdom and awareness IS Light — and the more Light you contain within your beings, the greater the sheen of your glow.

So surround yourselves, your homes, your computers, and your work places with crystals. Hold them and talk to them, and you will feel their consciousness being transferred to yours, and adding their Light and wisdom to yours, so that you can better access and understand the world around you, and glow like a beacon to your family and friends, who will feel the comfort of being near you — the comfort that you will radiate out to all in the radius of your energy field.

We spend so much time in our fields and forests, just basking in Nature's healing caresses, and feeling her lifestream pulsing through our veins. You, too, can feel this same pulsing of life, by spending more of your time outdoors. Now that it's Spring, you can sit and eat outdoors, as we do, instead of in your enclosed homes. This is the best relaxation there is and the best way to connect with Nature that there is — by being with her and not separated from her.

The Crystals, the Earth, and all lifeforms are One Consciousness. When you can understand and integrate this concept of Oneness, your life will gain a new flow, and synchronicity will be a common occurrence, as you will operate on a higher wavelength that re-connects you with all life everywhere; thereby allowing you to access all the avenues that will lead you to the fulfillment of your dreams on Earth.

I am Mikos, always dreaming of the day when we shall finally meet again, and embrace one another as friends from long ago. Know that I am always alert to your calls, and can guide you from my home underground, by your melding with my consciousness. This way, you will have double the help to guide you in your life. In fact, if you consciously stay within our frequency band, you will always find yourself exactly where you need to be, doing exactly what you need to do to accomplish your soul's purpose on Earth.

The Cetaceans communicate with each other no matter where they are in Earth's oceans, by staying in the frequency flow of "All That Is". It is the way the trees and animals and all of nature communicate. The first step is to be conscious of this interconnection of all life, and then you will find it flowing within you, with no "work" on your part. This is the key to the Universe, and it is within you. I am Mikos, and I bid you adieu. May your day be pleasant and beauteous, and your week filled with cheer.

Earth Is the Showcase of the Milky Way Galaxy

I reach out to you today, in harmony and goodwill toward all surface dwellers on Earth. We extend our friendship to you with open arms, to receive you into our lives, into our homes, and into the Inner Earth where we dwell. Harmony surrounds us all inside the depths of the Earth, and soon harmony will surround the entire Earth, as she rises in consciousness, as an ascending Star in the Heavens.

As Earth floats through space, her weary travelers climb the ascension ladder that will bring all souls into the knowingness of their beings. Due to the enormous amounts of energy being directed to Earth, a flame has been ignited in the hearts of mankind, a flame so great, that all humanity has caught the fire of God's spark of consciousness blazing in their hearts. This Light is awakening mankind to the remembrance of who they are, and the knowledge of the Universe contained in each tiny body cell.

We see the Light as it pours forth onto Sacred Mother Earth's body, igniting her atmosphere into a blazing Light that penetrates the body cells of all life on her surface. We, too, feel the intensity of this Light as it revs our vibration to speeds beyond Light. All on Earth are being blessed by the luminous Light show as Earth's aura gleams through the density that once kept her hidden in darkness.

Now her Light is seeping through the vast expanses of space, where all eyes are focused on her amazing birth into Light. She is ignited and fanned by God's Love, and all Ascended Beings, Angels, and Cetaceans carry the torch of Love that keeps her Light blazing through all life everywhere. No one can escape her Light now. Even the darkest of souls, who refuse to budge in their positions of power and destructiveness, are feeling the Light invade their space to reveal their intent to control the Earth's populations. They love the dark, and the Light is exposing all facets of their true character for all to witness. This is creating an uncomfortable environment for them, and causing them to step up their operations and react more intensely to situations in government and politics. They will do themselves in, and bring about their own demise.

Don't get caught up in the news or the skirmishes between the Light and dark that are erupting. For they will reach a crescendo and then decline and fade away, as these souls will finally step down from their positions of power and be removed from the Earth, never to reappear again. Their time is up. And yours, dear brothers and sisters of Light, is just beginning. Soon the Earth will have a new beginning. A beginning free of coercion, where every species will thrive through Unity Consciousness, and be able to bring all their dreams to fruition. It is the dream of life, and it is soon to be the norm.

We are all in for exciting times ahead, as all knowledge that has been kept from you will be revealed. You will bask in the Light of "who you are", and remember your purpose for being here. As Unity Consciousness envelopes the Earth, she will rapidly rise in frequency to burst through the third dimensional barrier of density into the Light of the fifth dimension, carrying you all with her.

These are remarkable times, never before experienced on Earth. **Soon you will be discovering hidden ancient knowledge, tablets and ancient writings that will remind you all of your heritage, and free you from life's struggle.** All you need is free.

We, in the Inner Earth, are free people living free lives. And this freedom is what keeps us perpetually young in heart and young in body. For we have resolved to never deviate from God's laws. For it is God's laws that keep us in health and wealth, and that perpetuates our life spans.

All is quickening on Earth. In the Inner Realms, where all is Light and all is Love, we watch in amazement as more and more humans awaken to the call of their souls daily, and opt for peace, opt for life, opt for all that is their birthright. The Earth is the Showcase of the Milky Way Galaxy, for it is bringing all life back to the heart of God, to be reunited in one great Wave of Ascension.

We remain hidden in the Earth's core until Unity Consciousness prevails on the surface, at which time you will find us in the midst of you, guiding you and loving you and welcoming you home. I am Mikos, speaking to you from the Library of Porthologos, where I am the Head Librarian.

19. Confederation of Planets

We Are An Arm Of The Creator

Dear Readers, I am Ashtar, from the United Confederation of Planets, division of the Ashtar Command, which circles your galaxy and solar system. We are part of the great brotherhood and sisterhood of Light for this part of the Milky Way Galaxy. We oversee your sector of the galaxy and solar system, and protect you from any outside intrusion intending to interfere with your evolution.

We protect you from the outlying reaches of space, where there are still pockets of dark forces that would like to overtake your planet for the wealth of resources it contains, including the human. There is a great war between the light and the dark coming to an end, and we in the Ashtar Command know of a certainty that this final battle is about to wage its last death throes leaving the earth and humans free to evolve. We watch over your skies and make sure that you are always protected as this darkness plays itself out until it just evaporates and disappears forever. We are the great forces of Light, and our cosmic assignment is to protect you always, to make sure that you regain your freedom so that you can evolve in peace and prosperity forevermore.

We are here as an arm of the Creator, maintaining peace in your sector where your solar system resides as you circle the galaxy in your everlasting trip around the sun. Soon you will be in a new position in the galaxy, one in which there is great light and brotherhood of solar systems. Where there is immediate connection of thoughts and vision, and where all are aware of each other, regardless of which planet you reside on. All work together in brotherhood of peace and love. This is what you are moving into. And this is what we are moving you toward. We will meet you there, in your new home position, where you will be able to freely and visually see and converse with us. So just look up to the sky, and visualize our star ships hovering above you and capturing you on our monitor screens. We know where each and every one of you are, always. We work together as one.

The Great Rebirthing Process

Greetings from the Space Command. I am Ashtar, your brother from the Stars, and I am with you this day of great earth activity, bringing you news of the great rebirthing process taking place on planet earth.

Unbeknownst to your physical senses, great amounts of energy are catapulting to Earth, bringing all life into greater attunement with God. Your scientists and astronomers are unaware of these events, for they base their work on outer occurrences of concrete evidence that they can gather and physically prove.

The shift that is taking place on your planet is the shift from Outer Consciousness to Inner Consciousness, away from travel to Outer Space and into travel to Inner Space. This is where the Great Exploration takes place. This is where you will find all the answers you are looking for.

> **"So, make this shift with us in consciousness, for it is where we all await you."**
> Ashtar

Are All Planets Hollow?
Know that there's life on all the planets in your solar system. These are your brothers and sisters living in a higher dimension than you, and whose electrons are vibrating at a greater velocity. Your electrons will soon pick up speed, and will be spinning at a rate that will propel you into the fifth dimension of Light, where we all await you.

For your information, **you are all living on a HOLLOW EARTH.** Your brothers and sisters who reside on other planets in your Solar System are also living on planets whose cores are Hollow. **All planets in your solar system are Hollow, with life both IN and ON them.**

Your sun, Helios, has a Hollow core, as all suns do. The light emanating from your sun is cold, not hot, as you have been taught to believe. It only reaches a higher temperature when it comes in contact with your atmosphere. All celestial bodies are Hollow, as this is the way they are formed. It is time that these truths were brought to earth!

We, in the Galactic Command, travel to all the planets in your Solar System, and are able to see them firsthand. Soon, you will have the capacity to travel to the other planets, and witness their true structure as well. Just know that all you've been led to believe will be open to dispute as you rise in consciousness.

Our Computer System Links Us to the Confederation
I am Adama. Know that the Confederation of Planets works closely with the inhabitants of the Hollow Earth and Telos. Know that we are in constant communication with them through our Computer Systems. Know that we monitor the whole Earth surface and below the surface.

Someday soon, you will have access to this vast computer system that's based on amino acids, and you will be able to plug into our vast monitoring network in the Cosmos. Then you will have the information and guidance you will need to stay in a state of balance and harmony with the Earth. This is all waiting for you, waiting for the energies to bring you and all life forms into the necessary state of consciousness that will allow us to implement this grand plan of bringing forth to you our vast computer system that will network you to the Stars.

We Trees Are The Ground Crew

We trees are here in service to the Ashtar Command, too. Only we are the "ground crew" who have "dug in" and live in our "dugouts," so to speak, while doing the same job and having the same assignments as you, who walk on foot and travel on land. It's just that our "physicality" is stationed in one spot, while our leaves blow hither and yon in the wind, and our scent and voices travel far inland.

For we communicate with all living life on the surface, just as you do. Our boughs reach through many dimensions as we stand guard on earth, and we are privy to information coming in on different wavebands also. Our auras are vast and connect us to one another across space, and we span earth's globe and hold her tightly within our auric arms of green and gold. We bless the earth, for she has given us life, life to reveal our innermost natures and life to express our selves in so many myriad ways and forms.

For as you walk, we talk, and our voices ever follow your footsteps, guiding you on your path through nature's innermost realms where you can play and experience the magic of our species, albeit, in different forms.

This is 'My Tree' in my backyard who channels messages to me, and when I sit under her branches, she becomes an extension of me, and is my antenna to the stars.

20. Ascension

Earth is Shifting into Higher Dimensions

We have only your highest good in mind. All we think is the goodness we feel in our hearts for all of humanity. Your Earth is shifting into the higher dimensions at a rapid pace, and your loss of time is your confirmation of this shift. Notice how quickly your days pass. Disregard the negativity you read about and hear on the news. It is the last stand of the dark forces, as they rear their heads in one last battle to dominate the Earth. Their time is over. A new Earth is dawning, a new sun is rising, and a new heaven is at hand. A glorious time is approaching. It is the freedom you all dream of, being birthed into your present.

In the Hollow Earth, heaven is all we experience, and if there were clouds we would 'walk on them' as your saying goes. Soon, you too, will feel the exuberance of 'walking on clouds', as your clouds literally fade away and your atmosphere 'lightens' up as the density dissolves and the pollution decreases, to bring your clarity of mind into focus as the new heaven descends upon your Earth plane and you, at last, can touch the stars.

So much is happening at levels you are not consciously aware of yet, to bring you all fully into the Light and back into the Confederation of Planets.

Earth has not been lost. On the contrary, its been saved by the Lightworkers who are emitting more and more Light daily, and the company of heaven who have dedicated their lives to raising Earth into the higher vibrations.

All Life Forms are Opting for the Ascension

All life forms presently on Earth are opting for the ascension. However, some will ascend with the Earth and with us at this time, and the others who have been unconscious of their inner choices and unwilling to ascend at this time, will do so at a later time. Know that the Earth's ascension is assured, and that we will all be moving our location closer to Helios, our Sun.

The people in the Hollow Earth are overjoyed with the rise in frequency that has taken place over the last few years. We yearn to connect with you in the physical, and now this connection is fully assured. We can even "guarantee" this, as you would say above. Yes, you are above us, but depth of location is irrelevant. **For with peace coming to the planet, all life will be assured of rapid evolvement to make up for the lost days of darkness.**

Humanity has learned its lesson well, and has learned the futility of war and bickering, and cries now for an end to the insanity. And the end is coming. You are witnessing the last eruptions on the surface.

From this point on, you will begin to see the merging of peoples, places and principles, as all come together in **ONE UNITED EARTH**. This is the day God has been waiting for. This is the day your holy God Selves have been praying for. This is the day we will open up the tunnel exits and come to you, with our brightly colored robes and sparkling sandals, bearing gifts of immense riches and the necessary devices that will return your planet to its pristine state once again, **for we can solve all your pollution and sickness problems in just moments.**

Timelines for Earth's Ascension

Today we will speak about the timelines for Earth's Ascension. Know that there are vast amounts of Light flowing to Earth from the Great Central Sun and beyond, including all Universes in our multi-universe system. All systems, everywhere, are aware of what is now occurring on Earth, and all are sending their support in the form of light waves. All these light waves are converging onto Earth's atmosphere and funneling into every cell of every life form on Earth, including our Earth herself. This is a spectacular revelation for beings on Earth to comprehend, and a spectacular sight to witness. All density is being lifted, felt, and dissipated into the ethers forever, transmuted to light, never to return anywhere again.

As all this is occurring, you are imperceptively being lifted higher and higher into the light frequency that you left when you came to Earth. Your bodies are being renewed and regenerated at a level you do not physically feel, and yet it is occurring moment by moment, until such a frequency is reached that you will suddenly explode into the diamond light that you are. It is all about reaching critical mass and timelines. The timelines for all this to occur, are closing in on your Earth, and converging from every direction and dimension, until they all close in upon one another and explode into NOW. And then you are there! There with Us in consciousness, and there with all life, located everywhere in all universes simultaneously. What an event to be able to witness, let alone be a part of as you all are. This has never been done before, anywhere in all existence. This is why there are vast numbers of beings from great numbers of universes here, circling your Earth, watching all this happen, and waiting for the great moment of synthesis to occur. And when it does, there will be great rejoicing throughout all the multiverses and beyond.

It's all about timelines and consciousness reaching a critical mass, and then everything takes off exponentially at a speed beyond anything you could conceive. The speed happens at a now moment, with no time elapsing at all. Ah, the wonders of God's creation.

Wait out the remaining timeline patiently, knowing that all will come to a glorious conclusion of instantaneous awakening for all life on Earth, jettisoning you all up to the stars, and down to us, of course.

Solar Flares

Today we will talk about how you are being bombarded by solar flares from your sun. This is all in anticipation of the new day dawning on Earth, the new day when all life will be free. The solar flares are burning away the negativity that is concentrated in the hearts of mankind, so that your heart energy can finally be freed to rise to connect you to your God Selves that wait patiently just a few feet above your heads. This is all part of the Divine Plan to free humanity from the grips of darkness that have enshrouded your Earth for eons. So look to your sun as your savior, for its light is purifying your planet as it gives you its warmth.

Critical Mass

Today it is calm in the Hollow Earth, as it is on all days, except for this special day of Sunday, as we wait for you to take our dictation. On these Sundays, there is a special breeze in the air, a breeze of anticipation as we connect with you again. It is as if the whole Hollow Earth stirs, knowing that it is time for us to deliver our dictation to you. It is a knowingness that pervades our air and we are all aware of it. So here you sit, with all our energies surrounding you, as you take our dictations. Our whole library knows of these Sunday channelings, and everyone sends their love to you.

You are so surrounded by our love. Our hearts are connected to yours, and we are ready to begin.

Greetings from the Library of Porthologos. Today the flowers are in mighty blooms of reds and purples, and their scents are wafting through our nostrils with the most delicious of fragrances. We pass these fragrances on to you, and hope you can capture their scents as you sit above us at your computer. We bring you good tidings and blessings of love from all the people in the Hollow Earth. More and more of us here below, are connecting with more and more of you above. It is indeed a wondrous time, in which all the prophecies are about to be fulfilled in this 7th golden age on earth. All of humanity are desiring peace, and people are waking up now by the thousands. There are now over 29 million surface humans awakening to who they are, and the critical mass that we are hoping to reach before 2012 is 55 million. With this critical mass achieved, we are assured of the 10,000 years of peace. It is also this critical mass that allows the Ascended Masters to visibly and physically walk the Earth surface, to openly teach the Universal Laws to mankind. So there are great changes ahead, and the changes all point to peace.

We in the Hollow Earth are pleased beyond anything we can express. For all these humans awakening, points to our soon being able to emerge from our homes beneath the earth, and physically join with the Lightworkers on the surface, where we too, will be teaching humanity the Universal Laws of life. All life on Earth is preparing to ascend, and help is coming from planets and star systems of which you don't even know exist. When people start questioning, and asking themselves the universal question of "who am I", then it is a sign of awakening, a sign that their soul is longing to know, longing to remember again. And once this question is asked, even though it is just a whisper, this gives the Ascended Host the opportunity to step in directly and begin teaching on a conscious level. But until people ask this profound question, we cannot directly help them. And once this question is asked, the whole universe jumps in to respond, and this person is added to the 'list' of awakening ones.

Know that we in the Hollow Earth know everything that transpires on the surface. We know the results of your presidential elections, and we are amazed at how the American people were so easily deceived and lied to, and how little they questioned the election process.

Our love for surface humanity goes deep, and we wish we could be on the surface now, giving our love and support to those lightworkers who are in need of us. For down here, we don't ever work or live alone, we always have our circle of friends, or groups, that we work with. These groups are our main support systems, and we work and travel together. This is what is lacking on the surface. Your families are all splintered and separated, and you have lost your group support system, which is crucial to life. Imagine the joy and fun of working on projects together, and receiving constant support?

Our love to you pours forth from the center of the Earth, and spirals into your heart in blazing colors of the rainbow. As you sit at your computer, you can feel these heightened sensations of contact, just as we can feel yours. It's this stepping up in vibration that happens whenever we connect in consciousness. It is our dream to someday be sitting right here in this room next to you, planning our workshops and talks to the populace. The best way to reach people is by working together, and we look forward to working with you as soon as we are on the surface.

Quickening the Soul

It is I, Mikos, talking to you from my hidden chamber beneath the Earth, where I dwell in the Light of God and where all reside in love and peace.

Our journey here is almost over, as the Light descends on you, our surface brothers and sisters, gradually bringing you all up to our frequency. When your light quotient reaches our frequency in intensity, we shall all instantaneously merge into **ONE GREAT LIGHT** from both above and below. It is at that instant that you will see us, as we emerge from our hidden homes underground. We are ready for this; it is the Quickening you've all been waiting for, and that Jesus talked about. It is the quickening of your souls to the Light – to quickly integrate the Light into your very own cells so that you shine as a beacon on Earth. All life everywhere in the Universe of Alpha and Omega, is waiting for this quickening to occur. It occurs by opening your heart flame to all life on Earth, especially those within your relationships. As this Light expands in you, it lights those you're connected to, and leaps as a hot ember from your cells to others in your proximity, thus igniting their cells simultaneously and expanding their Light. It is as if you were all standing in one gigantic bon-fire of light, and watching the flames as they flow into you and then out to everyone you come in contact with, including Mother Earth. It is a gigantic bon-fire of life, and you are throwing off sparks in all directions – just like fireworks; only these sparks catch and hold and integrate and expand, quickening the soul who is receptive to it.

Earth is creating quite a stirring in the Universe, for this time ALL of Earth will be ascending, igniting the 'domino effect' which will catapult this whole galaxy into the higher dimensions. It is the glory of God rejoicing. It is the Stars exploding, and it is your heart expanding into the One Heart of Creation.

Love Is The Key

Blessings my Sister above. It is Mikos, your brother from below, beginning this two-way session with you. Today we will talk about Love – Love for humanity that all people from below hold in their hearts for all people above. Yes, we hold immense, infinite Love in our hearts for all humanity living above ground. This is one of the purposes of our being here, to hold this love and constantly direct it to surface humans, so that the spark never goes out, but expands and expands until it ignites the spark within each of your hearts and explodes into the divine flame fully encompassing your beings with the light of the sun, that in that instant, brings you home to the heart of Creation.

All is love and all is light and all awaits your return journey home. Home is where the heart is – and the heart is the home of God – the eternal light of Creation.

Here in the Hollow Earth, our love is a stream of light that we send forth to quench your thirst and bathe your soul, until you yourselves can emit this light and connect it to ours. Once this occurs, all Earth will go up in a flame, and ascension of all will occur. This can happen just as easily now as it can later. For love is the key. As you learn to unconditionally love yourselves and love others, your lives naturally evolve, with no effort involved. Love is the base. And from love, all goodness is created. It is the alchemists secret that turns everything you touch into gold. So stretch your hearts to encompass all the love we send your way, and in turn shower your loved ones with it so that it spreads through your families and friends and workplaces. Become a 'love shower' everywhere you go, knowing that you are giving God's love wherever you are. You are here now as messengers of God, carrying God's message of love and hope to all mankind. You are the Christ returned, you are the Second Coming. It is you, not we, who bravely volunteered for this Earth assignment to bring love and light back to the surface. You are the spiritual warriors here to eternally free Earth from the clutches of 3rd dimensional density, and release her into the current of Light that will return her to the spiral of evolution where she can climb upwards through Eternity, instead of being stuck in the same rut as she has for the past 12 million years.

We are so eager for you to join us, for your hearts are pure and we 'see' that you truly want only peace and wellness in your lives. Your calls go out to the Universe, where all of God's creation responds by sending love back to you.

21. Reunion—A Swift Journey in Consciousness

Your Journey Home

Greetings from the Library of Porthologos, inside the Hollow Earth Realm of love and light, peace and abundance unlimited. I am Mikos, and gathered around me are my fellow brothers and sisters, anchoring the energy for this channeling session. We are all so very excited whenever we meet for these sessions, for these sessions are the only avenue we presently have to get our messages up to the surface for dissemination. So we love you and bless you for your service to Earth in relaying our thoughts. For our thoughts carry the love vibration we have for the people of Earth, and our eagerness to assist you with the ascension process through our words of wisdom and guidance.

We are here to guide you in your inward journey home. The trip is all within and, therefore, free of expenses and free of travel arrangements. You just sit quietly, focus on Us inside the Hollow Earth, and we will guide you to discover the gems within your own soul. We will help you mine the resources of your Being so you may discover the wealth that dwells within you. So start your inward journey now. <u>**As you read the pages of this book, know that you have hooked onto our vibration, and we are fully aware of you.**</u> Call to us now as we know your frequency and will embrace you in our love. We will work with you from below, whenever you call to us from above. The words in this book automatically attune you to us, and from this attunement we become aware of your desire to be with us in consciousness. And through our intermingling consciousness, we will guide you on your journey home. We will work with all who call to us. When we make this heart connection, it solidifies our partnership to work

together on the Inner Planes and to offer you the guidance you need to make your jump in consciousness. Once this jump is made, you will find us here, where we have always been, only then you will be able to see us, and you will see that we've always been beside you, had you been able to look far enough.

Drama in Optical Illusion

We send you greetings of love from beneath your soil, which is our rooftop. You are residing on the roof of your home, rather than inside. It's as if you build a house, climb a ladder to its roof, and set up housekeeping. You will soon become aware of other planets in the Milky Way Galaxy, and see for yourself the humans residing on the inside of their home planets, leaving the outside surfaces barren and free. You will be taking this visual trip as your visual acuity sharpens and your optic nerve opens and responds to the rising energy coming to Earth. Grand visions are awaiting you all, as our solar system and galaxy are responding to increased increments of Light and Love pouring forth from the Great Central Sun of Suns, from Alpha and Omega, the Creators of our Milky Way Galaxy. Your vision will be unlimited – all density and veils will fall away, and you will see life in all creation as it is and not through the dense optical illusions you now experience. The veils are even now being removed from the corneas of your eyes, by ever increasing light waves emanating from the Great, Great Central Sun. You will dance yourself into ecstasy as your vision unfolds and the stars and planets come into your sight and you focus and move into them as if they were just a stone's throw away – as indeed they are—only your vision has been blocked by your negative programming and illusion of being separate and apart, rather than connected and intertwined with all life in existence.

My, you are in for a great surprise! And we in the Hollow Earth can hardly wait to see the look on your faces as we make eye contact with you from our inner depths to your outer surface, and watch you blink in amazement as you look back into our eyes and laugh in excitement as you realize we were here the whole time and you just didn't see us. What a wondrous time is in store for us all, as we all finally connect and merge our consciousness into one.

It is all over, Beloveds. The struggling and pain are over. It was never meant to be. And as deep as you fell, your rise will be rapid, and you will make up the time lost, and excel in your evolutionary journey and raise your level of consciousness to great heights in only moments.

The script is already written; you are now just playing out your parts. But as the "drama" quickens, you gain momentum and carry the act to its divine conclusion with a "stand-up" audience applauding and cheering your bravery and stamina in the longest drama in illusion ever enacted. The curtain closes and you return home. It has ended.

We wait to receive you in our homes of crystal and gold, and treat you to our sumptuous meals and walk hand-in-hand with you through the Hollow Earth, treating you as the Queens and Kings, Goddesses and Gods that you are. We await your visit.

Message to Dianne

You are a direct descendent of us and have chosen to incarnate on the surface to bring our two worlds together. We are the Inner Earth Beings, and we are working directly with you and many others on the surface. We are imparting our knowledge of existence to you on a subconscious level, where you will have direct access to it as your vibratory rate increases. We will converse with you whenever you call on us.

We understand your yearnings and desire to be in contact with us, but know that you spend much time here in your dream state. You walk among us, and converse freely with our people while your body rests in your bed. You are attending our centers of Higher Learning. We are working with you in your sleep state, and consider you our representative on the surface.

Our lives are tranquil and peaceful, and this tranquility gives us the opportunity to evolve rapidly, and to delve into whatever sources of study we wish to learn. This is the purpose of life – to ever evolve in an environment where all have access to the myriad wonders of the universe.

Know that we keep our Inner Earth safe, and are vigilant and caring individuals. We regret the monstrosities that are occurring on the surface, and we lament the state of affairs and horrendous acts of killings in the Middle East and elsewhere. If we were to intervene directly, what could we do, and who would listen to us? We could come to your aid, but only the Lightworkers would accept us, and the rest of humanity would turn against us. Therefore, we remain "inner" ground, just as the Telosians remain underground at this time. We are hoping to come to your aid at the time of the great merging of our many civilizations in the different strata of Earth. Only God knows this timing, and the Spiritual Hierarchy guides us all unerringly.

We remain your brothers and sisters even though you have little contact with us, much less than you've had with the subterranean cities. They are the advance guard, so to speak, with us following. So stand guard over your Earth, and maintain your Light and center of gravity at all times, then nothing will blow you away from your mission to reunite all of Earth's peoples. We are the group consciousness of the Inner Earth Beings, and we love you and admire your tenacity to endure the above conditions. Blessings, our brothers and sisters.

KNOW WHO YOU ARE
KNOW YOU ARE ON
A GREAT GALACTIC MISSION
KNOW WE ALL TRAVEL BESIDE YOU AS ONE
ASHTAR

Crossing Over Dimensions

Our lives are so totally free compared to yours. We fly, while you crawl. You are all blessed to be on Earth at this time, as this is the crucial crossing over of dimensions leading to a new world of Light and Love for Earth. All of life is anticipating this crossover, and millions of Beings from other worlds are here witnessing it. You are all going on this journey together. There will be no further interference in the evolution of humankind, thus giving everyone the opportunity to ascend in the minimum of time necessary. Your Earth has asked the Spiritual Hierarchy to speed up the process of evolution so that all can begin a swift journey in consciousness.

22. How to Connect with Us

Universal Linkage

Greetings, our Brothers and Sisters of Light. We reside inside your precious Earth, ever ready to communicate with you. We have been here for hundreds of thousands of years, waiting for this glorious day to appear, when we could begin our communications with you on a regular basis. The time frame is now. All, whose intent is pure, can now connect with us through your heart flame, for we have the same flame in our heart as you do. It is the one flame of the Creator's divine spark of life. We are all connected through our heart flames, lighting up the world by our linkage. As we turn our connections on with each other, our auras become generators and transmit our light out into the universe where all can see it. We exponentially light up our whole Earth. This is what our oneness does – it lights up the Earth, carrying it to a higher level of consciousness which, in turn, moves us all higher up the ladder of evolution until we are catapulted into the next dimension where we will find ourselves automatically linked to everyone and everything. Our heart's connection is the key that opens up the universe and lets us in. And once in, we are forever united in consciousness as ONE. So as you connect to us, you connect to everyone, everywhere, through us. This is how universal linkage works. So link with us as we link with you, and you will be linked to the stars.

We Have Established a Link in Your Area of New York

I am Mikos, speaking to you from the Library of Porthologos, inside the Hollow Earth, beneath the Aegean Sea. We are gathered around you now, sending you our Love and our deepest longings for reunion with you and surface folk. We have established this link with you in your area of New York, to connect us with your part of the country. We have done the same in other locations, so that when the time for our emergence comes, we will have specific persons in specific locations that we can 'physically' contact. This is most important at this time, as our emergence becomes more and more possible as each week passes. So we humbly thank you for meeting with us each Sunday, as this link strengthens our connection with each channeling session. We leave you for now, and will continue our dialogue next Sunday. We send you our Love, and bolster your heart with our energies through the week between our channeling.

Points of Emergence
Questions and Answers

Q: How many locations will you be emerging from?
A: Know that there are many, many locations on the planet that are designated as Points for our Emergence. We will not elaborate on them all, as there are just too many. Points of emergence, of course, are entranceways that open up onto the surface from below, from where we will emerge. They are all camouflaged at this time, and some of them have not as yet been designated. Some entrance points will change in time. We are still in the process of clearing tunnels that haven't been used, and clearing entranceways of piled up debris. Our points of Emergence will not be finalized until the day we emerge, to accommodate the swiftly changing mass consciousness on the surface, and to accommodate last moment contactees.

Q: Can you tell us where some of those entrance points are located?
A: There will be points of entry in every country on the Globe. We don't as yet know the exact locations until we know who the contactees are. Yes, Austria, Australia,

Switzerland, Greece and Germany are most definitely included; as is Mt. Shasta in California, Pacifica in California, Rochester, NY, Hawaii, Washington State, Illinois and Texas. As we have spoken before, the locations are just too numerous to name them all. But rest assured that we will be emerging around the Globe, and you can picture these points by imagining the Globe dotted with sparkling diamonds, and wherever you cast your gaze, you will see sparkling lights dotting the landscape. These lights are our entrance points on the surface, camouflaged until the very moment of our appearance.

Q: How can one 'sign-up' to be a contactee in these locations?
A: Just ask, and you are chosen. It is that simple. Know that nobody is ever chosen for anything. Everybody chooses themselves for whatever it is that they want to participate in. This is Universal Law. So when someone asks to be a contactee, that person already has been chosen, by the very act of asking the question.

Q: How do I know if there is a Point of Emergence where I live?
A: Know that if you ask to be a contactee, your locality is then designated as one of our Points.

Q: What will be the signs of your Emergence?
A: When the time for our emergence is ripe, there will be many signs for you to heed. You will 'feel' our presence surrounding you, and your sense of 'feeling' that you are about to be contacted will heighten. You may even hear our thoughts as we try to reach you telepathically. But rest assured that you will clearly know that we are about to embark on our trip up to the surface.

Q: After one has 'signed-up' to be a contactee, what would be the duties prior to and after the physical contact with your people?
A: After one has 'signed-up' to be a contactee, all the information and responsibilities that this person will need, will be given in the dream state, and ready to access when we begin our emergence. They are like 'codes' that will fire off at the precise time, so that each person, in each locality, will know exactly what to do, how to do it, and when to do it. You will know everything you need to know, and the information will reside within your etheric body, where it will be safely kept until the exact time of our emergence. You don't have to do any 'thinking' about what your tasks or responsibilities will be, for you will be inner-directed and inner-guided, and you will feel our presence, and feel our guidance, coupled with your inner codes firing the information to your outer mind at the exact moment necessary. All that you need to accomplish your task as one of our contactees will be already within you.

So rest assured that you have nothing outwardly to do to prepare for this time, when you will be helping us by serving as one of our contactees.

But you do have something inwardly to do to prepare for this time, and that is to open your heart and feel our love streaming to you; merge your heart with this current of love, and connect with it in your heart space. We ask all who read these messages to do the same, whether or not they have volunteered to be one of our contactees.

Q: Where will you live when you come to the surface?
A: I AM **ADAMA** speaking to you on behalf of our people from the **SUBTERRANEAN CITY OF TELOS**, located beneath MT. SHASTA in CALIFORNIA, USA. Mikos suggested that I answer this question.

We greet you on the dawn of our emergence unto the surface of Earth. We have waited long for this day, and now it is here. We from below are fully ready for this momentous and grand emergence unto your surface lands and into your houses, where we hope to be welcomed by all. We know your love and light will make us feel right at home. Now we have some business to take care of. Know that there will be many thousands of us emerging from below, and we will all need homes to stay in. So we are asking those Lightworkers from above, who would like to volunteer and open up their homes to us, to please let us know. You can do this by calling on Mikos in the Hollow Earth or myself in Telos, and sending your thoughts stating that you wish to open your homes to us when we appear on the surface in the <u>very</u> near future. This will help us greatly in formulating our individual plans and preparing for our trip to our new homes upstairs. We thank you for taking this communiqué. I AM ADAMA.

We Hope You Will Hasten To Our Call

Our hearts are lit up with the joy of our connection with you this day, and the joy of knowing that all our words will go out to the masses on the surface so that they will know that their condition is reversible and can be changed in a moment into beauty and Light. The health of all life on Earth is dependent upon this connection into your inner beings, into the connection with the Spiritual Hierarchy of Earth, the Subterranean Cities of Light, and We, in the Hollow Globe.

Your mental and emotional health is dependent upon this connection, and your survival is dependent upon your connection with all life forms; especially the trees, who beckon and call to you and yearn to speak with you. Flow yourselves into us, as we flow ourselves into you, and this mighty ocean will flow this whole Earth into the fifth dimension of Light.

We bid you adieu, our brothers and sisters on Earth,
and hope you will hasten to Our Call,
for Our Call is also Your Call from Within.
It is all the same Call.
It is the ONE CALL from the Mighty Creator
calling us all home.

All planets,

In all Universes,

Will only evolve now…

Forever eternally evolve…

23. Earth's Glorious Future

Mikos speaks through Eric Karagounis

Stick Around

"We are meant to live in joy, and learn only from joy. Many of you on planet Earth at this moment are Starseeds, and not originally from Earth. You have volunteered to incarnate as Earthlings many times so you can be prepared for this final time. You are members of the "Family of Light". You are here to firmly anchor Light onto the planet. Your work is honored by so many Beings in the Universe, that you will wear the colors of gratitude for eons to come. The colors of your Auric Field will say "I Was There". No matter where you travel in the Universe, you will be flocked by Entities wanting to find out how it was done. How did you lift the Earth out of the darkness and turn her into a Star. For the next two thousand years, she will be the brightest Star in the Milky Way. Her Goddess Essence will illuminate our part of the Universe. Her rays of Light will carry the language of Love — the one true emotion of creation. She will become the main hub for our Galaxy. She will become a Living Library that will attract Beings from the outer reaches of the Universe who are seeking knowledge in order to enhance their evolution — knowledge that can only be accessed by the Human experience. Every experience is unique, but the Human experience holds the keys to ancient information of many Star Nations that worked together to seed the Earth with the best their civilizations had to offer. Hence the saying 'every Human is perfect'.

In the past, many Galactic civilizations had given up on her. But not the Family of Light. They knew deep within their souls that Earth was a gem they could not afford to lose. So they swung into action, and devised a plan that was so brilliant it even caught the attention of Prime Creator. You are on Universal television. And the ratings have become so high that millions of civilizations have put their evolution on hold to see the final episode.

So stick around, because after the final episode we are throwing a party of Galactic proportions. Every Being that has ever walked on planet Earth will be there. And if you think that we from the Hollow Earth look different, just wait till you see what's coming. Forever, Mikos and friends."

To all of you who read this book
From all of us in the Hollow Earth
We wish you a speedy journey
In raising your consciousness
To merge with ours…

THANK YOU
FOR TRAVELING WITH US
to the
CENTER
OF
THE
EARTH!

24. Addendum

TELOS is a Subterranean City located inside the enormous cavern of Mt. Shasta in California. Its citizens are survivors of the sinking of the Lemurian continent that occurred about 12,000 years ago. Their isolation from the surface population has enabled them to create a civilization of peace and abundance, with no sickness, aging, or death. The word 'telos' means "communication with spirit." Telos is one of over 120 Cities of Light that are only a few miles beneath the Earth's surface. As a grouping, these are called the 'Agartha Network.' (author)

About the City of Telos

Greetings from Telos! I am Adama, Ascended Master and High Priest of Telos, a subterranean city beneath Mt. Shasta in California. I am dictating this message to you from my home beneath the Earth, where over a million and a half of us live in perpetual peace and prosperity.

We are human and physical just like you, except for the fact that our mass consciousness holds thoughts of only Immortality and Perfect Health. Therefore, we can live hundreds and even thousands of years in the same body.

We came here from Lemuria over 12,000 years ago, before a thermonuclear war took place that destroyed the Earth's surface. We faced such hardships and calamities above ground that we decided to continue our evolution underground. We appealed to the Spiritual Hierarchy of the planet for permission to renovate the already existing cavern inside Mt. Shasta, and prepare it for the time when we would need to evacuate our homes above ground.

When the war was to begin, we were warned by the Spiritual Hierarchy to begin our evacuation to this underground cavern by going through the vast tunnel system that's spread throughout the planet. We had hoped to save all our Lemurian people, but there was only time to save 25,000 souls. The remainder of our race perished in the blast.

For the past 12,000 years, we have been able to rapidly evolve in consciousness, due to our isolation from the marauding bands of extraterrestrials and other hostile races that prey on the surface population. The surface population has been experiencing great leaps of consciousness, in preparation for humanity to move through the Photon Belt. It is for this reason that we have begun to contact surface dwellers to make our existence known. For in order for the Earth and humanity to continue to ascend in consciousness, the whole planet must be united and merged into ONE Light from below and ONE Light from above.

It is for this reason that we are contacting you; to make you aware of our underground existence so you can bring the fact of our existence to the attention of our fellow brothers and sisters above ground. Our book of channeled messages from Telos is written to humanity in hopes that they will recognize and receive us when we emerge from our homes beneath the ground, and merge with them on the surface in the not too distant future. We will be grateful to you for the part you play in helping us broadcast the reality of our existence.

Secrets of the Subterranean Cities
by Juliette Sweet

The Agartha Network
Think of Shamballa the Lesser as the United Nations of over 100 subterranean cities that form the Agartha Network. It is, indeed, the seat of government for the inner world. While Shamballa the Lesser is an inner continent, its satellite colonies are smaller enclosed ecosystems located just beneath the Earth's crust or discreetly within mountains. All cities in the Agartha Network are physical, and are of the light, meaning that they are benevolent spiritually based societies who follow the Christic teachings of the Order of Melchizedek. Quite simply, they continue in the tradition of the great mystery schools of the surface, honoring such beings as Jesus/Sananda, Buddha, Isis and Osiris...all of the Ascended Masters that we of the surface know and love, in addition to spiritual teachers of their own longstanding heritage.

Why did they choose to live underground? Consider the magnitude of the geological Earth changes that have swept the surface over the past 100,000 years. Consider the lengthy Atlantean-Lemurian war and the power of thermonuclear weaponry that eventually sank and destroyed these two highly advanced civilizations. The Sahara, the Gobi, the Australian Outback and the deserts of the U.S. are but a few examples of the devastation that resulted. The sub-cities were created as refuges for the people and as safe havens for sacred records, teachings and technologies that were cherished by these ancient cultures.

Capitol Cities
POSID: Primary Atlantean outpost, located beneath the Mato Grosso plains region of Brazil. Population: 1.3 million.

SHONSHE: Refuge of the Uighur culture, a branch of the Lemurians who chose to form their own colonies 50,000 years ago. Entrance is guarded by a Himalayan Lamasery. Population: 3/4 million.

RAMA: Remnant of the surface city of Rama, India. Located near Jaipur. Inhabitants are known for their classic Hindu features. Population: 1 million.

SHINGWA: Remnant of the northern migration of the Uighurs. Located on the border of Mongolia and China. Population ¾ million.

TELOS: Primary Lemurian outpost located within Mt. Shasta, with a small secondary city in Mt. Lassen, California, USA. Telos translated means "Communication with Spirit". Population: 1.5 million.

Spotlight on Telos
How can over a million people make their home inside Mt. Shasta? While we're stretching our imaginations, our neighbors, the Japanese, have already blueprinted underground cities in answer to their surface area problem. Sub-city habitation has, for thousands of years, been a natural vehicle for human evolution. Now, here is a peek at a well-thought-out ecosystem.

The dimensions of this domed city are approximately 1.5 miles wide by 2 miles deep. Telos is comprised of 5 levels.

LEVEL 1: This top level is the center of commerce, education and administration. The pyramid-shaped temple is the central structure and has a capacity of 50,000. Surrounding it are government buildings, the equivalent of a courthouse that promotes an enlightened judicial system, halls of records, arts and entertainment facilities, a hotel for visiting foreign emissaries, a palace which houses the "Ra and Rana Mu" (the reigning King and Queen of the royal Lemurian lineage,) a communications tower, a spaceport, schools, food and clothing dispatches and most residences.

LEVEL 2: A manufacturing center as well as a residential level. Houses are circular in shape and dust-free because of it. Like surface living, housing for singles, couples and extended families is the norm.

LEVEL 3: Hydroponic gardens. Highly advanced hydroponic technology feeds the entire city, with some to spare for intercity commerce. All crops yield larger and tastier fruits, veggies and soy products that make for a varied and fun diet for Telosians. Now completely vegetarian, the Agartha Cities have taken meat substitutes to new heights.

LEVEL 4: More hydroponic gardens, more manufacturing and some natural park areas.

LEVEL 5: The nature level. Set about a mile beneath surface ground level, this area is a large natural environment. It serves as a habitat for a wide variety of animals, including those many extinct on the surface. All species have been bred in a non-violent atmosphere, and those that might be carnivorous on the surface now enjoy soy steaks and human interaction. Here you can romp with a Saber-Toothed Tiger with wild abandon. Together with the other plant levels, enough oxygen is produced to sustain the biosphere.

LANGUAGE: While dialects vary from city to city, "Solara Maru," translated as the "Solar Language," is commonly spoken. This is the root language for our sacred languages such as Sanskrit and Hebrew.

GOVERNMENT: A Council of Twelve, six men and six women, together with the Ra and Rana Mu, do collective problem solving and serve as guides and guardians of the people. Positions of royalty, such as are held by the Ra and Rana Mu, are regarded as ones of responsibility in upholding God' s divine plan. The High Priest, an Ascended Master named Adama, is also an official representative.

COMPUTERS: The Agarthean computer system is amino-acid based and serves a vast array of functions. All of the sub-cities are linked by this highly spiritualized information network. The system monitors inter-city and galactic communication, while, simultaneously, serving the needs of the individual at home. It can, for instance, report your body's vitamin or mineral deficiencies or, when necessary, convey pertinent information from the akashic records for personal growth.

MONEY: Non-existent. All inhabitants' basic needs are taken care of. Luxuries are exchanged via a sophisticated barter system.

TRANSPORTATION: Moving sidewalks, inter-level elevators and electromagnetic sleds resembling our snowmobiles within the city. For travel between cities, residents take "the Tube," an electromagnetic subway system capable of speeds up to 3,000 m.p.h. Yes, Agartheans are well versed in intergalactic etiquette and are members of the Confederation of Planets. Space travel has been perfected, as has the ability for interdimensional shifts that render these ships undetectable.

ENTERTAINMENT: Theatre, concerts and a wide variety of the arts. Also, for you Trekkies, the Holodecks. Program your favorite movie or chapter in Earth history and become a part of it!

CHILDBIRTH: A painless three months, not nine. A very sacred process whereby, upon conception, a woman will go to the temple for three days, immediately welcoming the child with beautiful music, thoughts and imagery. Water birthing in the company of both parents is standard.

HEIGHT: Due to cultural differences, average heights of subterranean citizens vary — generally 6'5" to 7'5" in Telos, while nearly 12' in Shamballa the Lesser.

AGE: Unlimited. Death by degeneration is simply not a reality in Telos. Most Agartheans choose to look an age between 30 and 40 and stay there, while, technically, they may be thousands of years old. By not believing in death, this society is not limited by it. Upon completing a desired experience, one can disincarnate at will.

ASCENSION: Absolutely, and much easier and more common than on the surface. Ascension is the ultimate goal of temple training.

Why have they stayed underground all this time? In part, because the Agartheans have learned the futility of war and violence and are patiently waiting for us to draw the same conclusion. They are such gentle folk that even our judgemental thoughts are physically harmful to them. Secrecy has been their protection. Until now the truth of their existence has been veiled by Spirit. When can we visit? Our entrance to the sub-cities depends on the purity of our intentions and our capacity to think positively. A warm welcome from both worlds is the ideal and must be expressed by more than just the lightworking community.

Currently, a few hundred brave subterraneans are working on the surface. In order to blend with the masses, they have undergone temporary cellular change so that, physically, they don't tower above the rest of us. They may be recognized by their gentle, sensitive nature and somewhat mysterious accent. We wish to introduce you to Princess Sharula Aurora Dux, the daughter of the Ra and Rana Mu of Telos. Sharula has been officially appointed Ambassador to the surface world by the Agartha Network. She was born in 1725, and looks 30. This article is courtesy of her firsthand experience.

Printed with the permission of World Ascension Network/Telos Press, copyright 1993.

THE ASHTAR GALACTIC COMMAND
by Ashtar-Athena SherAn

The Ashtar Command is the airborne division of the Great Brother/Sisterhood of Light, under the administrative direction of Commander Ashtar and the Spiritual guidance and directorship of Lord Sananda Kumara known to Earth as Jesus Christ our Commander-in-Chief. We are also known as the Galactic Command, the Solar Cross Fleets and the Orion Jerusalem Command. We are the Hosts of Heaven who serve the Christ, our Most Radiant One, in His mission of universal love. We can best be understood as celestial or angelic in nature, functioning as councils of Light upon missions of Holy endeavor in accordance with the Divine plan.

As a member of the Galactic Confederation we oversee this sector of the Milky Way Galaxy protecting the Divine plan against any type of interference or violation of confederation Law or Melchizedek protocol. We are here to assist humanity through the current dimensional shifting in consciousness, the transformation of your physical forms into a less densified etheric-physical form capable of ascending with the Earth into the fifth dimension. We also work in coordination with our brothers and sisters in Telos and their Earth based Silver Fleets under Commander Anton and with the Melchizedek High Priest of Telos, Adama. We are all working together under the authority of the Office of the Christ, the Great Central Sun Hierarchy (Throne of God), and the Order of Melchizedek. We also have our bases located within mountain ranges, in desert areas and under the oceans. We, our bases and our Merkabahs (aerial chariots or starships), are invisible unless we wish otherwise. In order to see us your vibration would have to match the wavelength upon which we are manifesting. We, and our higher dimensional vehicles are composed of etheric matter, as real and solid to us as your environment is to you. Thus we appear by lowering our wavelength to match the third dimensional vibration and we disappear by raising our vibrations beyond your visibility range.

We would like you to know that you are not alone in the universe nor anywhere else for that matter. What you do affects not only your world but countless other civilizations and worlds existing in different dimensions but just as desirous of maintaining their existence as you are yours. In fact, Ashtars first personal entry into your solar system occurred in 1952 in response to urgent reports that Earth was attempting to detonate the hydrogen atom, a living organism, an act in violation of Confederation law. The state of the pollution and decline of your planet's ecosystem as well as your delving into nuclear fission for defense purposes caused him to immediately send delegations from the High Council of the Ashtar Command to meet with certain heads of your planetary government. We do all that is possible without violation of your free will to neutralize excess radiation within your soil and atmosphere and to deflect potentially dangerous asteroids from impacting your planet. We maintain the stability of your planetary axis and as much as possible relieve the pressure of your tectonic plate systems thus directing earthquake activity away from heavily populated cities. We constantly monitor all geophysical and astrophysical conditions affecting Earth as well as other planetary systems. We are universal ambassadors of peace, peacemaker/diplomats and peacekeepers, and we greatly anticipate the day when you too will join us within the United Federation of Peaceful Worlds.

The Ashtar Command is composed of thousands of starships and millions of personnel from many civilizations. We also have many members of the Command currently living on

Earth, some having been born into Earth families, and others who come and go, living for a time amongst their brothers and sisters on Earth and then returning to their respective points of cosmic origin.

Life upon Earth and throughout this solar system was originally seeded by the Elohim, so it is very similar if not identical in form. We are all Rays of the one God-Source-Creator and as such have the Divine duty and mission to extend God's love throughout all time and space continuums. It is you who give a face, voice and hands to God's love in your world. You are in the End Times, the last days of war, conflict and harmful intent. Sooner than you can possibly fathom, you and your precious orb will move into a kinder, gentler version of your world. It has simply outworn peaceless existence as a viable or allowable option. Within less than twenty years the Earth and all upon her will transform into a world of pure love. Those not willing or capable of making that transformative adjustment will find themselves in the world of their choosing.

The Divine Plan is always perfect and always just. Watch for the miracles occurring daily in your life and worldwide. These will continue until you realize that you are deeply loved and part of a plan more beautiful and wondrous than you could have ever imagined. We are sending you messages of love and universal truth via crop circles, designs ever more intricate and exquisite. We are even sending circles and cross patterns of light to adorn your buildings and glow in your windowpanes.

Please stop a moment and contemplate how you live and move and have your being within such a great God! Know that you are an embodiment of Divinity designed to be fully indwelt by the Holy Spirit. That is your real nature and calling in life and you will only find genuine and lasting joy and peace when you give unconditional expression to the love that you are. Ask, it will be quickened within you. Please also receive our love that we offer to each one of you upon your beautiful planet.

You may know us as your elder brothers and sisters, as the co-workers of Christ upon a mutual mission of love. We are the celestial heralds of the good news of God's love for all of His Creation and of the entering of your world into a higher dimension of understanding, revelation and life more abundant. In the Light of our Most Radiant One we bid you God's Blessings. Adonai, The Ashtar Command.

(The above message was transmitted through Commander Lady Athena, currently serving upon Earth and known as Ashtar-Athena SherAn. You may contact her by calling and leaving a message at 253.927.3739 or by emailing AthenaSheran@aol.com)

THE SMOKY GOD

A reprint of the 1908 classic by Willis George Emerson. This wonderful book tells how a Norse father and son sailed into the inner earth and spent two years there. The book describes the people, their religion and their sun.

The Smoky God is the real life account of a Norwegian sailor named Olaf Jansen. His story, set in the 1800s, is told in Willis Emerson's biography entitled "The Smoky God." Olaf's little sloop drifted so far north by storm that he actually sailed into a polar entrance and lived for two years with one of the colonies of the Agartha Network, called "Shamballa the Lesser." He describes his hosts as those "of the central seat of government for the inner continent . . . measuring a full 12 feet in height . . . extending courtesies and showing kindness . . . laughing heartily when they had to improvise chairs for my father and I to sit in." Olaf tells of a "smoky" inner sun, a world comprised of three-fourths land and one-fourth water.

$15 plus $5 s/h, credit card customers call 732.602.3407. Inner Light Publications, Box 753, New Brunswick, NJ 08903.

Admiral Richard E. Byrd's Flight into the Hollow Earth

Admiral Byrd said, in February 1947 before his North Pole flight, "I'd like to see that land beyond the Pole. That area beyond the Pole is the center of the great unknown."

On February 19, 1947, Admiral Richard E. Byrd left Base Camp in the Arctic and flew northward. What happened on that flight?

"During his Arctic flight of 1,700 miles BEYOND the North Pole he reported by radio that he saw below him, not ice and snow, but land areas consisting of mountains, forests, green vegetation, lakes and rivers, and in the underbrush saw a strange animal resembling the mammoth...."

"For years rumors have persisted that on his historic flight to the North Pole, Admiral Byrd flew beyond the Pole into an opening leading inside the Earth. Here he met with advanced beings who had a sobering message for him to deliver to mankind on the Surface World."

"Upon Byrd's return to Washington, on March 11, 1947, he was interviewed intently by top security forces and a medical team. Our government branded him as a lunatic and kept him drugged and locked in an asylum in the interest of national security."

Here, from Admiral Byrd's secret log and diary, is the message meant to have been heard 56 years ago!

Excerpt from *A Flight to the Land Beyond the North Pole*:
"I bid you welcome to our domain, Admiral." I see a man with delicate features and with the etching of years upon his face. He is seated at a long table. He motions me to sit down

in one of the chairs. After I am seated, he places his fingertips together and smiles. He speaks softly again, and conveys the following: "We have let you enter here because you are of noble character and well-known on the Surface World, Admiral." "Surface World," I half-gasp under my breath! "Yes," the Master replies with a smile, "you are in the domain of the Arianni, the Inner World of the Earth. We shall not long delay your mission, and you will be safely escorted back to the surface and for a distance beyond. But now, Admiral, I shall tell you why you have been summoned here. Our interest rightly begins just after your race exploded the first atomic bombs over Hiroshima and Nagasaki, Japan. It was at that alarming time we sent our flying machines, the 'Flugelrads,' to your surface world to investigate what your race had done. That is, of course, past history now, my dear Admiral, but I must continue on. You see, we have never interfered before in your race's wars and barbarity, but now we must, for you have learned to tamper with a certain power that is not for man, namely, that of atomic energy. Our emissaries have already delivered messages to the powers of your world, and yet they do not heed. Now you have been chosen to be witness here that our world does exist. You see, our culture and science is many thousands of years beyond your race, Admiral." I interrupted, "But what does this have to do with me, Sir?"

The master's eyes seemed to penetrate deeply into my mind, and after studying me for a few moments he replied: "Your race has now reached the point of no return, for there are those among you who would destroy your very world rather than relinquish their power as they know it..."

I nodded, and the Master continued. "In 1945 and afterward, we tried to contact your race, but our efforts were met with hostility. Our Flugelrads were fired upon, yes, even pursued with malice and animosity by your fighter planes. So, now, I say to you, my son, there is a great storm gathering in your world, a black fury that will not spend itself for many years. There will be no answer in your armies; there will be no safety in your science. It may rage on until every flower of your culture is trampled and all human things are leveled in vast chaos."

"Your recent war was only a prelude of what is yet to come for your race. We here see it more clearly with each hour...do you say I am mistaken?"

"No," I answered, "it happened once before, when the Dark Ages came and they lasted for more than five hundred years." "Yes, my son," replied the Master, "the Dark Ages that will come now for your race will cover the Earth like a pall, but I believe that some of your race will live through the storm; beyond that, I cannot say. We see at a great distance a new world stirring from the ruins of your race, seeking its lost and legendary treasures, and they will be here, my son, safe in our keeping. When that time arrives, we shall come forward again to help revive your culture and your race.

Perhaps, by then, you will have learned the futility of war and its strife...and after that time, certain of your culture and science will be returned for your race to begin anew. You, my son, are to return to the Surface World with this message..."

With those closing words, our meeting seemed at an end. I stood for a moment as in a dream...but, yet, I knew this was reality, and for some strange reason I bowed slightly, either out of respect or humility, I do not know which.

Suddenly, I was again aware that the two beautiful hosts who had brought me here were again at my side. "This way,

Admiral," motioned one. I turned once more before leaving and looked back toward the Master. A gentle smile was etched on his delicate ancient face. "Farewell, my son," he spoke, then he gestured with a lovely, slender hand a motion of peace and our meeting was truly ended.

Quickly, we walked back through the great door of the Master's chamber and once again entered into the elevator. The door slid silently downward and we were at once going upward. One of my hosts spoke again, "We must now make haste, Admiral, as the Master desires to delay you no longer on your schedule timetable and you must return with his message to your race."

Excerpt from: *A Flight to the Land Beyond the North Pole; The Missing Diary of Admiral Richard E. Byrd.* Admiral Byrd's lost secret diary that details his flight to beyond the poles into an actual opening that leads inside the Earth where he met masterful beings who keep track of our civilization.

$12.95 plus $5 s/h
Credit card customers call 732.602.3407.
Inner Light Publishing/Global Communications,
Box 753, New Brunswick, NJ 08903.

TELOS
The Call Goes Out
from the
HOLLOW EARTH
and the
UNDERGROUND CITIES

By Dianne Robbins

Telos is an ancient Lemurian City of Light that is real and exists to this day in the physical realm, underneath Mt. Shasta. Meet Adama, the High Priest of Telos, as he describes the kind of earthly paradise they have forged for themselves as they raised their consciousness to let go of all violence and negativity. Because they have moved into a consciousness of total love and true Brotherhood, it has been possible for them to survive from the time of the sinking of the continent of Lemuria until now. They have created Heaven on Earth for themselves in their Subterranean Cities and throughout the Hollow Earth. They are looking forward to coming out, when we are ready, to teach us how to do the same here on the surface.

This book is a must for those of you who are seeking your ancient roots and heritage. This book will open your mind and heart to the great possibilities and wonders that are awaiting us, on the surface, when we finally let go of the old paradigm of duality and discord, and turn to Love and true Brotherhood for all. This book brings all of us so much hope for a better and easier life here on this planet.

Explore the rich family life of the people from the lost continent of Lemuria, who have been subterranean for the past 12,000 years; and who, due to their isolation from the surface population, have created a civilization of peace and abundance, with no sickness, aging or death.

Read about the Advanced Civilizations that live in peace and brotherhood in the Center of our Earth, which is Hollow, and contains numerous physical cities of Light, its own Inner Central Sun, with oceans and mountains still in their pristine state. Vividly and heroically, Telos delivers a clear understanding of what is required on the surface to create a prosperous society and a healthy environment. The Telosians and other spiritually advanced civilizations do indeed exist inside the Earth, and they are coming forward at this time to inspire us to follow in their footsteps.

ISBN 0 9700902-0-X
Order from:

Dianne Robbins
Box 10945
Rochester, NY 14610 USA
585.802.4530
Email: HollowEarth@photon.net

http://www.DianneRobbins.com

$15.00 plus s/h: $4 USA, $4 Canada, $7 International

Thank you to Marina Tonti for translating and publishing my TELOS book in **Greek**. Anastasakis Radamanthis, Ideotheatron, Stournari 57 str, Athens, Greece.

Thank you to Martine Vallee and Ariane Editions Inc., for translating and publishing my TELOS book in **French**. 1209, av. Bernard O. bureau 110, Outremont, Qc, Canada H2V 1V7.

Thank you to Clara Macario, for publishing my books in **Spanish**. Pasaje El Cerro 3487, (1407) Capital Federal, Argentina.

The Call Goes Out:
Messages from the Earth's Cetaceans
Interspecies Communication

by Dianne Robbins

- A series of messages channeled from the Cetacean species — whales and dolphins.
- Graphically spells out why they are here on Earth, how they work with the Confederation of Planets, and how we interfere with their mission.
- Readers will have their eyes opened to the rich family and cultural life of another intelligent species on this planet.
- Contains messages from **Keiko, Star of the *Free Willy* movies.**

Dianne has been a telepathic channel for the Cetaceans in previous incarnations, and channels the ONE GROUP MIND of the Cetaceans. Since early on, she has been connected to the Cetaceans, and was an active member of Green Peace in the seventies.

In a personal message to Dianne, they expressed the following: "We are the Cetaceans, awake also at this early Earth hour, floating along with the currents and sending our love to all on Earth in their sleep state. We breathe the clean air as it comes in off the shore, where humanity hasn't yet polluted it with exhaust fumes from their automobiles and factories. These early hours are the sweetest and the cleanest time to breathe deeply, for the vigor of God deeply permeates the air at these early hours. Keep your heart space open to our transmissions; for although our species differ in form, in consciousness we are one".

"We are here in our full consciousness, waiting patiently for Earth's children to bloom into the Caretakers you were meant to be. Your DNA was tampered with by past civilizations and by renegades from Outer Space. This has slowed down your evolution to the point where up to now you were barely crawling. With the huge input of energy being directed to your Earth within the last few years, your evolution is again picking up speed, and you will soon blast off into full consciousness, and will at last be with us in the higher dimensions."

This work of attunement is also a call for help. Help required for the waste that is dumped into the oceans, for the melting of the polar caps due to air pollution, for destruction of the Rain Forests, and for our need to listen to the Earth and hear her messages. Indeed, the reader will find the insightful words of Keiko, Star of the *Free Willy* movies; Corky, an Orca Whale incarcerated in Sea World, San Diego, California; and Lolita, an Orca Whale, imprisoned in the Sea Aquarium in Miami, Florida, among others.

"Dianne Robbins, has brought us a masterpiece of compassion that should be required reading for all who care about our planet and our future." Richard Fuller, Metaphysical Reviews;
(616) 532-7299 www.metarev.com
6"x 9" Quality Paperback, 152 pages, ISBN 1-880666-64-2

The Call Goes Out: Messages from the Earth's Cetaceans

Dianne Robbins, Box 10945, Rochester, NY 14610, USA
Phone: 585.802.4530

http://www.DianneRobbins.com
Email: HollowEarth@photon.net

$13.00 plus s/h: $4 USA, $4 Canada, $7 International

About the Author

As a child, I used to stand outside and look up at the night sky, and wonder where, in the starry heavens above, was my home.

In 1990, when I was listening to the music of the Moody Blues and heard their song *"I Know You're Out There Somewhere,"* it suddenly flooded me with memories and I instantly knew there was a whole other world out there, just waiting to communicate with me. I began a process of meditation that reawakened me to the remembrance that I am a telepathic receiver and transmitter for the Inner-Earth terrestrials and Cetaceans. I also awakened to my divine mission and role for this lifetime.

I tapped into the cosmos and connected to the Cetaceans (Whales and Dolphins), Adama in the Subterranean City of Telos, Mikos in the Hollow Earth, the Ascended Masters, the Ashtar Command of the Confederation of Planets, Nature Spirits and Trees. I no longer felt alone, but suddenly connected to Beings everywhere through the telepathic phone lines that exist throughout the cosmos. My communication with Mikos has reconnected me to who I am, and why I am here, and **I discovered that I am connected to all life – everywhere – not just on Earth but all life throughout our Milky Way Galaxy.**

With this new sense of purpose, I have dedicated my life to receiving, transcribing, and publishing my telepathic transmissions from Beings residing in Higher Realms of consciousness. My goal is to spread these messages around the globe in hopes of awakening surface humans to the existence of those who inhabit the Hollow Earth and Subterranean Realms through the publication of my books.

The earliest messages came from the Cetaceans and were published in my first book: *The Call Goes Out, Messages from the Earth's Cetaceans.*

My second book and pre-requisite to this book is *TELOS, the Call Goes Out from the Hollow Earth and Underground Cities.*

Much of my inspiration comes from communing with nature through long walks in the woods, sitting under my favorite tree in my backyard, and walking along the ocean when I'm in Florida.

Dianne Robbins
Box 10945
Rochester, NY 14610 USA
585.802.4530

Email: HollowEarth@photon.net

http://www.DianneRobbins.com

Original Cover Design by James L. Michaelson.
Though his true passion in high school was singing and writing folk music (initially inspired by the Kingston Trio) it was his great talent in the field of art that would be the hallmark expression of his vocational life. Success came early in this regard, from his very first endeavor in the world of commercial art. A concert poster he rendered in the fall of '66 of a fledgling rock group call Jefferson Airplane became a tremendous retail "hit" and served as a catalyst for the formation of Sparta Graphics poster company around James and his creative abilities. Later successes using this form of art included many of the attraction posters, which remain on display at Disneyland to this day.

James was one of the creative core that initiated Landmark Entertainment in the early 80's. It was at this juncture that he developed skills and expertise in all areas of theme park design, illustration and master planning. For the next twenty years he enjoyed a fruitful career as a freelance artist again working with the likes of Disney, Paramount Parks and several other renowned companies worldwide.

His most recent fine art print, "Mt. Shasta - Rebirth of Innocence" is the first of many creations to come which express his true heart's desire for the manifestation of a new world where a greater truth reigns amidst a collaboration of beings where love, peace, joy and abundance abide. This recurring theme will be expanded upon throughout all of his "New Earth Visions". Included in these projects will be the soon to be released, second fine art print, "Heaven on Earth". Plans are also in the making for the release of a wondrous CD, as well as an illustrated book about "Middle Earth".

James L. Michaelson
Box 1108, Mt. Shasta, CA 96067 (530.926.6624)

25. Resources

Hollow Earth Researchers, Books, Web Sites, Art

Hollow Earth Researchers
Timothy Green Beckley, BRANTON (Bruce Walton), David Hatcher Childress, Jan Lamprecht, Rodney Cluff, Alec Maclellan, Raymond Bernard, Tal LeVesque, John Symmes, Edgar Rice Burroughs, Kevin and Matthew Taylor, Joseph H. Cater, Theodore Fitch, William R. Bradshaw, Sadek Adams, Marshall B. Gardner, Raymond Palmer, John Uri Lloyd, Sir Edmund Halley, William Reed, Amadeo Giannini, Cyrus Reed Teed, Max Fyfield, James Gilliland, Danny L. Weiss, and conceptual writers such as Jules Verne.

Hollow Earth Books
World Top Secret: Our Earth is Hollow, by Rodney Cluff; a 450 page e-book that is loaded with scientific and scriptural evidence about the hollow earth and its inhabitants. www.ourhollowearth.com

Hollow Planets, by Jan Lamprecht; living leading authority on hollow planets. This is a 600-page reference book packed with scientific data that will answer anyone's scientific questions on the hollow earth and beyond. www.hollowplanets.com

The Hollow Earth, by Raymond Bernard; engaging and popular book supporting the Hollow Earth theory containing a well defined outline as to what exactly the hollow earth is, and provides proofs to support his findings.

Agharta, The Subterranean World, by Raymond Bernard

A Journey to the Earth's Interior, Marshall B. Gardner

Phantom of the Poles, by William Reed.

Rainbow City and the Inner Earth People, by Michael X.

Subterranean Tunnels and the Hollow Earth, from World Explorer Magazine, vol. 2, no. 3, by David Hatcher Childress, (Adventures Unlimited Press, 815.253.6390)

A Guide to the Inner Earth, by Bruce Walton; a huge catalogue of manuscripts on the Hollow/Inner Earth.

Mount Shasta, Home of the Ancients, edited by Bruce Walton (BRANTON).

The Smoky God, or a Voyage to the Inner World, by Willis George Emerson; a real life story of a Norwegian sailor, and his journey into the polar opening of the Arctic. Having spent 27 years of his life in an asylum upon returning to the surface, Olaf Jansen kept his secret to his deathbed, when he shared his story and maps of a Hollow Earth filled with giants, with his neighbor Willis George Emerson, in Glendale, California.

Editorhpa, by John Uri Lloyd; a brilliant novel written in 1895 describing a journey into the earth. Fantastically illustrated.

Lost Continents and the Hollow Earth, by David Hatcher Childress with writings of Richard Shaver; this 344 page book is a thorough examination of the early hollow earth stories of Richard Shaver.   815.253.6390, Adventures Unlimited Press.

The Hollow Earth Enigma, by Alec Maclellan. Adventures Unlimited Press. 191 page book compilation of evidence that the Earth is hollow and populated.

The Land of No Horizon, by Kevin and Matthew Taylor; this 280 page book conveys scientific and biblical evidence on how the Inner Earth holds the secrets to the origins of humanity. www.tlonh.com

Hollow Earth Authentic, by Sadek Adam; a 100 page self-published book that integrates information from a variety of sources that authenticate that the earth is hollow. Printed in Great Britain ISBN-0-9534441-0-4

Subterranean Worlds Inside Earth, by Timothy Green Beckley. Inner Light Publishing, Box 753, New Brunswick, NJ 08903, 732.602.3407

Worlds Beyond the Poles, by Amadeo Giannini; this book contains the original press and radio releases of Admiral Byrd's discovery of subtropical vegetation, rivers and lakes over the North and South Poles.

Lands Beyond the Poles, by Ray Palmer, published by Gray Baker.

Becoming Gods II, by James Gilliland. Pages 145-151 in this book contain the author's research of the Earth being Hollow and inhabited. www.eceti.org 509.395.2092.

Hollow Earth In The Puranas, by Dean Dominic De Lucia. The Long-Overdue Vedic View of the Hollow Earth. TGS Services, 22241 Pinedale Lane, Frankston, Texas, 75763, 903.876.3256.   d_delucia@hotmail.com

Web Sites
www.DianneRobbins.com and www.onelight.com are the premier online sites of Inner Earth Resources. Here you will find Dianne's other books and links.

Adventures Unlimited Press www.wexclub.com/aup has a catalog of books about the Hollow Earth. 815.253.6390

www.hollow-earth.org is the web site for ISCE (International Society for a Complete Earth), organizing an expedition on the same route of Admiral Byrd to the North Pole entrance.

www.hiddenmysteries.com, for more books about the Hollow Earth. "Specializing in many hard-to-find, rare, and some out-of-print books which are on the 'official' suppressed books lists by many governments in the world". info@hiddenmysteries.com   903.876.3256

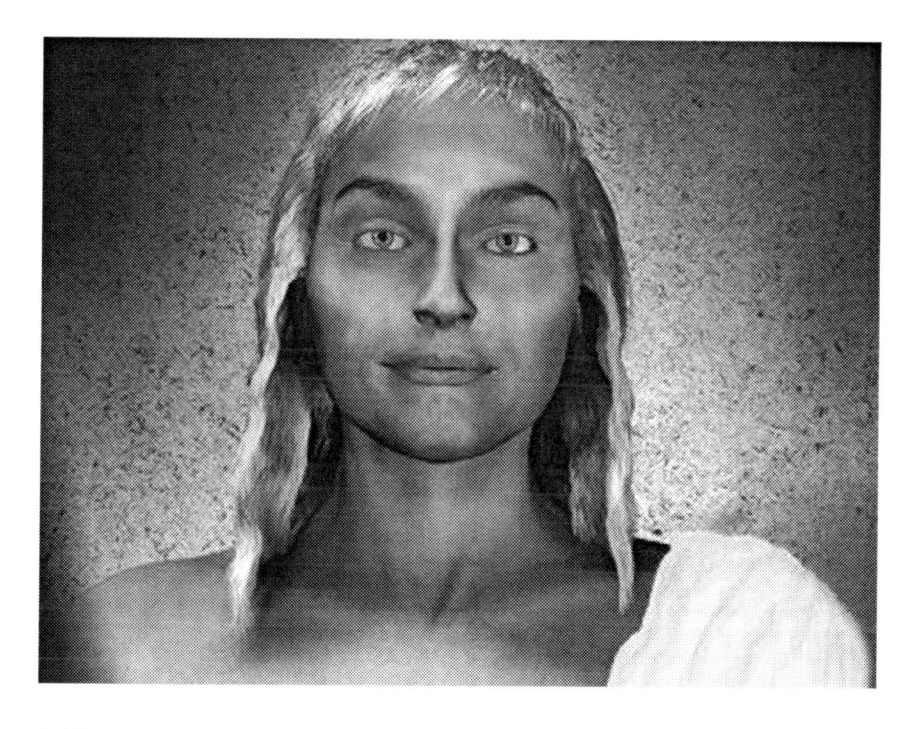

Mikos
Digital Art by Maia Christianne Nartoomid+
(see next page for contact information)

ART

SPIRITUAL GUIDANCE
AKASHIC INSIGHTS
SPIRIT-ART

Maia Christianne Nartoomid+

Maia has also created a portrait of Mikos!
Contact her to obtain your own
COLOR frameable portrait of Mikos.

Maia's ability to read the holographic recording crystals of the planet allows her to glean insights into your personal soul journey - past, present and future. These expanded perspectives have the potential to help you experience more of who you are and to better understand your soul's purpose for incarnation. Maia has done session work for the author of this book. Contact Maia for your session today!

Spirit-Art Offerings
Spirit Art Prints - Commissioned Art Work
Maia created a portrait of Mikos in this book!
**Contact her to obtain your own
COLOR frameable portrait of Mikos.**

Maia is co-founder of:
Spirit Heart Sanctuary
415 Dairy Road, Ste. E. PMB 149
Kahului, HI 96732
505.424-1052
www.spiritheart.org
krystos@spiritheart.org
Also Visit Maia's Akashic Spirit-Art Website
www.spiritmythos.org

Mikos of Porthologos
(Artist Greg Gavin's drawing of Suzanne Mattes Bennett's visual description of her meeting with Mikos)

Greg Gavin
onelighta@yahoo.com
http://www.onelight.com

Portrait of Adama
By Visionary Artist Glenda Green

Further information about Glenda Green's visionary artwork can be found by going to:
www.lovewithoutend.com

To view a portrait of Adama, and Rosalea who is an Elder in Telos

see the **TELOS** book at

www.DianneRobbins.com

Dianne Robbins:
Box 10945
Rochester, NY 14610 USA

585.802.4530

HollowEarth@photon.net